THE GROOM WORE BLUE SUEDE SHOES

Jessica Travis

Silhouette

ROMANCE™

Published by Silhouette Books

America's Publisher of Contemporary Romance

To special friends who helped along the way:
Barbara Veillon, Barbara Colley, Kent Conwell,
Lela Davis, Rogayle Franklin, Susan Wingerd and
Janet Milkovich.
But, especially to my daughter, Chaney, who introduced
me to *Lou*, and Jim, my real-life hero.

 SILHOUETTE BOOKS

ISBN 0-373-19143-X

THE GROOM WORE BLUE SUEDE SHOES

Copyright © 1996 by Jessica Roach Ferguson

"You don't like me, do you?"

Travor challenged. "Or is it Elvis you don't like? I haven't quite figured it out."

Erin felt her face burn. Obviously the guy hadn't picked up on her attraction to him. Good. She didn't need to get hung up on a man who looked like Elvis Presley. There would never be any peace in their lives.

"I want to know what your game is," she said, conveniently changing the subject.

"My game?"

His innocent expression riled her. "Look, you've fooled a lot of people, but you haven't fooled me. You're too good. You're too perfect. Every movement, every nuance is just too Elvis-like. Now what do you want?"

Travor smiled and eased his arm around the back of the sofa. Then he pulled her toward him and kissed her.

Dear Reader,

Spring is on the way—and love is blooming in Silhouette Romance this month. To keep his little girl, FABULOUS FATHER Jace McCall needs a pretend bride—fast. Luckily he "proposes" to a woman who doesn't have to pretend to love him in Sandra Steffen's *A Father For Always*.

Favorite author Annette Broadrick continues her bestselling DAUGHTERS OF TEXAS miniseries with *Instant Mommy*, this month's BUNDLES OF JOY selection. Widowed dad Deke Crandall was an expert at raising cattle, but a greenhorn at raising his baby daughter. So when he asked Mollie O'Brien for her help, the marriage-shy rancher had no idea he'd soon be asking for her hand!

In *Wanted: Wife* by Stella Bagwell, handsome Lucas Lowrimore is all set to say "I do," but his number one candidate for a bride has very cold feet. Can he convince reluctant Jenny Prescott to walk those cold feet down the aisle?

Carla Cassidy starts off her new miniseries THE BAKER BROOD with *Deputy Daddy*. Carolyn Baker has to save her infant godchildren from their bachelor guardian, Beau Randolph. After all, what could he know about babies? But then she experienced some of his tender loving care....

And don't miss our other two wonderful books— *Almost Married* by Carol Grace and *The Groom Wore Blue Suede Shoes* by debut author Jessica Travis.

Happy Reading!

Melissa Senate,
Senior Editor

Please address questions and book requests to:
Silhouette Reader Service
U.S.: 3010 Walden Ave., P.O. Box 1325, Buffalo, NY 14269
Canadian: P.O. Box 609, Fort Erie, Ont. L2A 5X3

JESSICA TRAVIS

considers herself a late bloomer. Until she married Jim, became a stepmother to his son Brian, and gave birth to their daughter Chaney, she had no idea what life was all about.

Born and raised in Longview, Texas, Jessica's an avid collector of everything, especially friendships. There's nothing she enjoys more than helping other writers try to reach their goals.

During the past fourteen years, because of her husband's work, Jessica and her family have lived in Gonzales, Baton Rouge, New Iberia, Luling and Lake Charles, Louisiana, as well as Houston, Kingwood, Port Neches and Sugar Land, Texas. If her nomadic life-style brings her to your town, don't hesitate to say hello.

Dear Reader,

Funny how ideas come to a writer. Most of mine originate from my family—from some quirky reaction or observation they make. *The Groom Wore Blue Suede Shoes* came about when my daughter, Chaney, became obsessed with Elvis Presley.

We were sitting in a hotel room in Baton Rouge, Louisiana. Chaney was only four, but when she saw Elvis singing and dancing to "Jailhouse Rock", she was instantly captivated. Always an Elvis fan, I never reached the point of obsession, and here my sweet little girl had me wondering what I'd missed. And that's when the Elvis phenomenon hit our house!

I read everything I could get my hands on—the good, the bad and the ugly—out loud. We watched every Elvis movie and documentary—more than once. It was fun. It's *still* fun. We each learned a lot about Elvis's world and his faithful fans. This book is about them, and for them.

The Groom Wore Blue Suede Shoes is my first book and is very special to me, my husband and my daughter because it's a combined effort.

I hope you like Travor, Erin, Lou and Max. Most of all, I hope you laugh.

Jessica Travis

Chapter One

"Hey, Mom! Look at those women tearing the clothes off that guy!"

Erin pulled into the parking area beside a huge red-and-black tour bus, slamming her foot on the brake of her custom van just as two screaming females darted in front of her.

"Look! They're fighting over his shirt!" her son yelled.

The glaring bright lights of a fast-food restaurant joined forces with the other artificial lighting, making the scene before her hazy. She squinted her eyes. Leaning over the steering wheel, she saw people inside the restaurant, pressed against the windows, peering out and pointing. A hundred yards away, a man was running for his life while trying to gently fight off his attackers. Something about him seemed vaguely familiar.

"They must be making a movie," Max stated, sitting on the edge of his seat.

Erin looked around the parking lot. "I don't see a camera crew. Besides we would have heard about it."

"Who is he, Mom? Someone famous?"

"I can't tell, but anyone that famous is a fool to try to get a burger in a popular place like that...if that's what he was doing." She drew her attention away from the fugitive and fumbled for the coupons inside her purse.

"Look at him go! Jeez, look at that guy go!"

Erin did look. Through the haze of semidarkness, all she could see were wild women, screaming and clawing at bare skin. She'd seen it before, numerous times during her growing-up years. She'd even been a part of it—not willingly, of course.

She studied the scene before her, glad to be a safe distance away. The stranger didn't seem to be very aggressive when it came to defending himself. He appeared to be trying to reason with his attackers. Erin thought she could see his mouth moving, although his features were shadowed by a baseball cap and jaw-length black hair. She caught herself willing him to take off the cap and beat the screaming women away. He didn't. Instead, he twisted and turned, presenting a shadow show for the onlookers.

"Something's not right," Erin spoke aloud.

"What, Mom?"

She wrinkled her brow. "If he's such a well-known celebrity, what's he doing here alone? Maybe it's a publicity stunt."

They both looked around for hidden photographers, waiting to snap some superstar being assaulted at a fast-food joint. They saw no one who even resembled a reporter or a cameraman. "Poor guy. If he's looking to be discovered and staged this scene, I'm afraid he got more than he bargained for," Erin said.

Suddenly, the stranger broke away from the crowd of women and with a fresh surge of energy ran as fast as his long legs could take him across the asphalt. His bare arms flew up and he pulled the bill of the cap lower onto his forehead.

Just as suddenly, the few onlookers—mostly men and children—boomed through the doors of the restaurant and on to the adjoining playground. Erin watched as one beefy young man shimmied up the clown and attempted to take a picture of the fleeing celebrity. An older man fought off the teenager who was trying to get up the slide first. The senior citizen won, and he, too, poised his camera for the best shot.

Max jumped up from the passenger seat and moved to the center of the van.

"What are you doing?" Erin called after him.

"We gotta help him, Mom, even if he did do this on purpose."

"Don't be ridiculous!"

"Drive up beside him, Mom, and I'll open the door. He can just dive right in."

"Max, don't open that door. This isn't your grandmother you're with tonight. You know I don't believe in—"

"Look, they're gaining on him! He doesn't have a chance!"

Sure enough, the women were in fast pursuit and it seemed they'd grown in numbers. They were hysterical, reaching out to him almost desperately. Erin shuddered.

Maybe I should help. Maybe the guy's plan back-fired and he's alone, at the mercy of his so-called ad-mirers. She didn't envy him one bit.

Quickly, she surveyed the situation. If he darted out onto the busy boulevard, he'd be struck down within seconds. His only hope was to run the length of the parking lot over and over again until either he or his fan club dropped from exhaustion.

Or until they caught him.

The thought prodded her into action. She released her foot from the brake and eased forward on the gas pedal. She cautiously trailed the comical parade of females.

Hesitantly she passed them, praying one wouldn't leap in front of the van. Max slid open the side door while Erin accelerated and pulled up beside the panting stranger. They still couldn't make out his face. The bill of his cap was pulled low, hiding his features and the mass of black waves around his ears was in total disar-ray.

"Jump in," Max yelled. "Come on, mister, jump in."

Erin watched in horror as a bright red boot-shoe came out of nowhere and struck the stranger just as he lunged for the door. She was even more horrified when his head landed solidly against the side of her bucket seat. He tottered precariously, half in and half out of the van. As if that wasn't enough, the women trailed thickly near the door, screaming, crying and shouting obscenities. One spike-haired redhead reached out and grabbed the stranger's foot; she war-whooped trium-phantly when a shoe came off in her hand. Encour-aged, her followers picked up speed and relieved the man of his other shoe and both socks.

Max grunted, tugging desperately on the limp body. Erin reached out and grabbed the man's arm, pulling with all her strength while maneuvering the van toward the boulevard. Miraculously, there was a break in traffic. Erin cut to the right. "Hang on to him, Max! Don't let him slide out!"

She succeeded in avoiding the barrage of screaming, hysterical women who were shaking their fists at her.

"I got him!" Max yelled. He wrestled two long legs, bent them at the knees, then slammed the sliding door shut. He seemed to be in complete control.

Erin breathed a sigh of relief. She was anxious to get away from the mob. She didn't condone such nonsensical behavior. Still, she acknowledged her own interest as to the identity of this fugitive celebrity. Her heart beat sporadically, much like it did years ago when her mother chased Jerry Lee Lewis through the streets of Shreveport, Louisiana. And there were other times just as bad.

Looking in the rearview mirror, she prayed the crazed fans wouldn't hop in their cars and give chase. She made a few unnecessary turns ... just in case.

"Max?" she whispered. She dared not take her eyes from the highway. When there was no sound from the back seat, she glanced in the rearview mirror again. "What's wrong?" she asked. "Are you okay, Max?"

Max rose from his position astride the stranger, stepped over the prostrate form and threw himself into the passenger seat. "I'm okay, Mom, but he's out cold. Did you hear his head crack the side of the seat? Who do you think he is? I never did see his face."

Erin shook her head in exasperation. "I guess we'll find out soon enough. From the actions of that mob, I'd say we've got someone super hot on our hands."

"I don't know, Mom. I think he mumbled something about being buried back in Texas."

Erin frowned. "That was a song. Maybe he's a country-western singer." She shook her head again. "Whoever he is, he's learned a valuable lesson."

Max nodded. "Yeah. I'll bet he won't stop for any more burgers."

She glanced at her son, arching an eyebrow. "That's not exactly what I was thinking."

Fifteen minutes later, they turned silently into a circular drive. Erin shut off the ignition.

"Max, you go turn off the security system, then go in Grandma's bedroom and get the baseball bat from behind the—"

"Aw, Mom. He's out. He's not gonna hurt us."

"We don't know that this guy's a celebrity. What if he snatched someone's purse? What if he tried to rob the restaurant? That might be why all those people were after him."

"Women, Mom. Women were after him," her son corrected. "They were fighting over his shirt. Swiping his shoes and socks. You've seen Grandma do it a thousand times. They were after souvenirs."

Erin gritted her teeth. "Humor me, kiddo. Go get the bat."

She watched Max fiddle with the alarm system, then enter the house. Suddenly she felt very alone. She could almost feel strong hot fingers encircling her neck and squeezing the life out of her. Quickly, she got out of the van and slammed the door. Walking around to the passenger side, she waited for Max to return. She didn't want to tackle the stranger alone. He could easily overpower her. Not that her eleven-year-old small-for-his-age son was any protection, but the baseball bat was.

The guy could be playing possum, waiting for them to open the door. What if he really was some gangster type? *We should have gone straight to the police department,* she thought.

Max raced through the screen, banging it against the side of the house. He was empty-handed.

"Where's the bat?" Erin asked.

"Oh, I couldn't find it."

"Max, you go back and—"

"Have you looked at him yet?"

Erin tried to grab his arm as he raced past her, but he swerved out of her reach and pulled the van door open before she could object. Two bare feet fell toward him, followed by two long legs.

"He's still out. Come on, Mom, help me."

Against her better judgment, Erin grabbed one leg while Max took the other. The faded denim felt soft from numerous washings, and Erin noticed the edges of his pant legs were worn. He usually wears boots, she thought. Oddly, her heart fluttered a little faster. They tugged and pulled until his naked back became visible. They gasped.

From the glare of the floodlights installed around the house, Erin could see what adoring fans were capable of. Scratches ran deep from his shoulder blades to his waist. Blood was smeared, still oozing.

"We'll have to get him inside the best we can," Erin stated from between clenched teeth. "He's going to need some first aid."

The stranger groaned, seemingly agreeing with her.

"C'mon, mister. Help us. Get on your feet and we'll take you inside," Max urged.

Erin was always taken aback by her son's take-charge personality. He was definitely a leader, just like his grandma.

"Help me, Mom."

She slipped her arm beneath the man's stomach. She was temporarily stunned by the warmth of his skin and the prickly feel of coarse hair. He was damp with perspiration. Erin couldn't help but notice how firm and solid his stomach felt. A fleeting picture of a weight lifter flashed through her mind. They wrestled him out of the van and her heart leaped when his cap fell to the ground. She was one step closer to his identity. They maneuvered him to a standing position. He was a big man and clumsy, she supposed from the blow to his head.

"Easy, mister," she suggested, for lack of anything better to say. "You're going to be okay."

He was almost a foot taller than Erin and beneath the weight of his arm, she couldn't crook her neck to look up at him. The three of them hobbled toward the house.

"Okay, Max, he's handling his own weight. Run ahead and get the first-aid kit. Take it to Grandma's room."

Max sprinted away, glancing back as he reached the door. He stopped abruptly and Erin saw his eyes bulge in surprise and his mouth drop open. God, she hoped the man's face wasn't as scratched up and bloody as his back. "Hurry, Max," she called.

The stranger leaned more heavily on her. Erin was sniffing the intriguing mixture of sweat and masculine after-shave when she realized what she was doing. She held her breath. They were almost to the door.

"Just a few more steps," she encouraged, but as soon as they crossed the threshold, he stumbled forward and fell through the entrance, pulling her down with him.

"Get off me!" she yelled, throwing his heavy arm from around her. She wiggled across the floor and turned to swear at the fugitive, but nothing came out of her mouth.

The scene before her was startling. His face was turned away from her; his black hair was thick and askew. The bloody stripes down his back glistened. He didn't move.

Erin wished desperately for a weapon, something to help her defend herself and her son if the need should arise. She swallowed, forced herself to once again speak to the man. Her voice was a whisper. "Okay, fella, let's try it once more."

He didn't respond, and Erin wondered what she should do.

"Look, are you okay?" She crawled toward him, leaned over him and hesitantly brushed at the shiny black hair that hid his face. She drew back in horror and swallowed hard at the lump in her throat. Finally, she found her voice, but it came out hoarse and grainy. "Dear God! Don't you have better sense than to show up in Memphis!"

The absurdity of her words stunned her. He couldn't be who she thought he was.

"It's Elvis. It's really him, isn't it, Mom?"

Erin jumped as if Max had shouted the words. Her heart pounded in her chest. "No, of course not."

It can't be!

Max took a hesitant step toward her. "Yes, it is," he argued in a low voice.

She turned to look at her son. His eyes were huge in his small, pale face. The freckles on the bridge of his nose seemed to be marching. He had that same anxious look her mother always got right before she zeroed in on a superstar. "He's bleeding, Max. Apparitions don't bleed."

Max walked closer. "He's not a ghost. I don't believe in ghosts. He's been hiding out just like the newspapers said. It was really him they saw in Michigan, and now he's come home."

Erin looked down at the stranger. It would be easy to let her imagination zoom along with her son's. The tousled black hair and long, thick sideburns were definitely Elvis-like. The ruler-straight nose was like his, too. And although she could see only a profile, she could tell from the one closed eye that his lashes were so dark they appeared to be dyed and outlined with black mascara. She shook her head and reined in her imagination. "He's one of those impersonators," she whispered. "A look-alike, Max, right down to that gaudy diamond ring."

He has to be!

Max didn't respond and Erin turned her attention back to him. She'd never seen her child look so shaken. She touched his arm. "Max, you've seen hundreds of them with your grandma. They're a dime a dozen in August. You know that. Besides, this guy's too young." The look on her son's face told her he wasn't convinced. "Come on, let's try to drag him into the bedroom and get those scratches taken care of."

They stood over him, hesitant to touch him. Although Erin knew he was flesh and blood, warm and firm, she visualized reaching for his arm and watching her hand disappear, just like a hologram.

He's human. He's not a ghost. He's human. She silently repeated the words twice for luck, then grasped his arm. Max followed suit and together they managed to get the stranger to the bedroom.

He seemed to belong in the pink-and-black surroundings. Or was it just Erin's imagination? She stood over him, dabbing at the scratches with antiseptic-soaked cotton. He was tan, smoothly perfect, except for the wounds inflicted by his fans. She corrected her thought. *Not his fans. Elvis's fans. This guy isn't the real thing.*

But what if he is? her mind screamed. What if there's been a cover-up?

Don't be a fool!

She dabbed ointment liberally and searched her memory for some recollection of the real Elvis Presley's back—moles? Scars? Birthmarks? She couldn't remember.

"Wonder why he's so out of it?" Max asked, interrupting her thoughts. She'd forgotten her son, who was watching her closely.

"I don't know. Surely he didn't hit the car seat *that* hard. I wonder if we should call a doctor. I think he should have a tetanus shot."

They continued to whisper as if waking the stranger would confirm their suspicions or worse, negate their hopes.

"Boy, wouldn't Grandma have a fit? We need to call her."

"Oh, no, we don't." Erin rolled her eyes at Max. "Thank God, she's not here. We don't have the finances for another one of her Elvis brainstorms. We just can't afford any more mistakes." She put her hand on Max's shoulder. "Besides, we never know what Lou would do. She'd either kill him for impersonating 'the King' or she'd keep him as a souvenir with the rest of this junk.''

Both Erin and Max looked around the bedroom decorated in *his* favorite colors. Elvis Presley movie posters obliterated the walls. The drapes appeared to be made of nothing more than Elvis buttons. Lou Weller had every piece of Elvis memorabilia she'd been able to get her hands on, and her entire house proved it.

Our new home, Erin thought. While Lou was in Hawaii, paying homage to the memory of Elvis, Erin and Max had moved out of their apartment and into the Weller house. It was financially necessary if they wanted to continue to operate the little music studio over on Poplar Avenue. And you can guard our collection, Lou had told them. It didn't matter that her expensive security system would curtail a burglary; that the numerous outlandish floodlights on the modest ranch-style house would intimidate a thief. Lou didn't plan on losing Elvis—in any way, shape or form—again.

A groan from the bed brought their attention back to reality. The man was coming to. Erin stepped away from him; Max leaned over him.

"You okay, mister?" he whispered.

"Home... Gotta get home..." the man mumbled.

Goose bumps prickled over Erin and she rubbed her arms roughly.

"You are home, mister. We're just a few miles from Graceland."

"Max!" Erin hissed.

Her son grinned sheepishly and shrugged. "Just testing him, Mom."

Erin frowned. "Don't go getting flaky on me. Your grandma's got that market cornered."

"Home..." the man mumbled once again.

Gathering her courage, Erin neared the bed and leaned over him. His skin was tanned from the sun and she could almost visualize him working shirtless on a chain gang. She pushed the thought aside, determined to give him the benefit of the doubt. Besides, she thought, he needed help. They had to rescue him.

She studied his profile carefully. He looked healthy, wholesome. If he was a bad guy, wouldn't he have a harshness about him? she wondered. Wouldn't there be some telltale sign of wickedness, meanness? She couldn't resist brushing the hair away from his face, or caressing a bushy thick side burn with her forefinger. Something quivered in the vicinity of her heart and she pulled away. "Just sleep. Rest for now and we'll get you home later," she promised.

The stranger visibly relaxed. Mother and son tiptoed out of the room.

"What are we gonna do with him?" Max asked, walking toward the big-screen television, searching for the remote control. He found it and flicked it on, but adjusted the sound to Mute.

"We're not going to do anything with him," Erin stated. "At least, not right now." All she wanted at the moment was silence.

Unfortunately, Max had other plans. He dropped to the floor at her feet. "The newspapers were right. He's been recuperating from some mysterious disease and now he's—"

He stopped midsentence when Erin shook her head.

"You explain it, then," he challenged.

Erin took a deep breath. "He's an impersonator. It's all so clear and simple. Those people at the restaurant came in on the tour bus—you saw the bus. They probably came to see Graceland, and all the Elvis hangouts. They were programmed for Elvis and when this dude walked in—well, it's obvious what happened. They went wild.''

Max grunted as if he didn't like his mother's theory.

"Grandma says that Elvis was frozen and that he's coming back when he—"

"Oh, Max, you know your grandma is Looney Tunes when it comes to Elvis.''

"She has some good ideas, Mom," he argued.

"Not very often. And we're at a point where we can lose every cent we have. The house, the studio. We're going to be living out of that van if we're not careful.''

"We're not that broke. Grandma went to Hawaii and she couldn't have done that if we were really broke.''

Erin shook her head. How could she explain it to him, that she didn't have the heart to cancel Lou's annual pilgrimage to Hawaii? But this is the last trip. She shook her head again, and said the words aloud. "This is the last trip.''

Max jutted out his chin and Erin could see a combination of herself and Lou in his thin face. "Grandma knows exactly what she's doing. We're gonna be rich.''

Erin sighed. "The subject is closed, Max." She put a hand on his shoulder and squeezed. "We never did get to eat. Want to go in the kitchen and finish off those leftovers?''

He made a face. "We've eaten them three times already. Anyway, I'm not hungry. I'll just wait and eat with El—" He glanced at his mother. "The stranger," he corrected, and grinned.

Erin shot him a warning look and settled deeper in the bucket-style chair. She wasn't hungry, either. Her stomach was still doing flip-flops and her mind's eye was playing and replaying her first glance at that side-burned profile. She closed her eyes to better capture the memory. She was on the verge of reaching out—in her mind—and touching silky black hair when Max's excited shouts brought her out of her reverie.

"Mom, look, look!" He pointed the remote control toward the television and turned up the sound.

"Oh, no," Erin groaned and sat forward on the edge of her seat. The broadcaster's voice boomed at them.

"Unlike the scene of the Michigan sighting, today's individuals were armed and ready. Having arrived only moments earlier aboard a Tucson, Arizona, tour bus, several people were carrying cameras and camcorders."

Erin groaned again as she watched a blurry reenactment of what she'd personally experienced.

"When suddenly, a white van appeared out of nowhere and rescued Elvis...."

"It's us!" Max yelled.

The amateur cameraman had focused just enough to show the figure of Max standing in the door of the van.

"It's me!" he yelled again, more excited this time.

Erin watched in horror as the red boot-shoe, so vivid in her memory, sailed through the air and hit the running man. She winced. But what she saw next released a prayer from her lips. The cameraman zoomed in closer and the license plate of her van slammed before her eyes.

"God help us," she whispered. "They've got us now."

Chapter Two

Travor opened one eye. He closed it tightly, then opened it again. He squinted. Elvis Presley was standing in the corner of the bedroom.

Gently raising himself to his elbows, he peered around the room. Not in his worst nightmares had he seen anything like this. Cardboard Elvises were standing in every corner. Movie posters papered the walls. Travor quickly closed his eyes. The atrocious pink-and-black decor was slightly nauseating.

Successfully fighting off a wave of sickness, he sat up but stared at the floor to keep from facing the six-foot rock and roller before him. Where the hell am I? he wondered.

The skin across his back felt tight and tender, and his head pounded. His wrists burned. He glanced down at them and was startled to see scratches glistening with some kind of clear goop. He sniffed but it was odorless. His watch was gone. Then he remembered the raging women and his heart leaped to his throat. Had they captured him? He glanced around the room again as he ran a hand through his thick black hair.

That's odd, he thought, noticing his bare feet. He wiggled his toes just to make certain the feet were his. Nothing seemed real in this room. Hell. Nothing had seemed real since he'd hit Memphis. He wondered if he was dreaming.

Again the horror of being chased by a mob of women entered his memory and he put his face in his hands, more from embarrassment than anything else. He could just imagine how he'd looked loping across the restaurant parking lot with a herd of women after him. He'd been very aware of the onlookers; even people in cars on the street had been rubbernecking. I never should have turned off on Elvis Presley Boulevard, he thought.

Travor rubbed the back of his neck and studied the museum surrounding him. He shook his head at the cardboard figure.

A noise from another section of the house got his attention. He tilted his head and listened. It sounded like voices.

Still dazed, he got to his feet and glanced around for his shirt. *No shirt.* He ran a hand over his bare chest as he made his way to the door and eased through the hallway. He turned to the right and stopped, holding his breath.

A boy was on his knees on the floor, pointing toward a big-screen television set. A young woman was on the edge of her seat; she looked tense. She was definitely upset about something. Travor turned his eyes to the screen but all he saw was some guy holding up a can of dog food. The sound had been turned off.

No one was aware of him standing there. The woman was frantically running her fingers through chin-length white-gold hair. Then suddenly, she stood, reached for her purse and pulled out a set of keys. Her faded jeans hugged her calves, but the rest of her petite figure was hidden by a blousy, oversize shirt.

The kid reached for the keys. "I'll put it in the garage, Mom. Don't worry, they won't find us."

Mom? I would've pegged her as his big sister. A surge of disappointment raced through him. *Damn. Where there's a kid, there's usually a father.* Still, a quiver penetrated his stomach just as the boy's words penetrated his mind. *Fugitives? What have I gotten mixed up in?*

"Turn off the floodlights, Max, so the neighbors won't see you. Everyone has probably seen the newsbreak by now."

Her voice was breathlessly husky. The quiver in his stomach intensified.

"Mom, Mrs. Tillotson next door knows we have a white van. The entire neighborhood knows."

"We'll worry about that later," the woman answered.

White van? He remembered a white van. *Jump in, mister. C'mon, jump in.* The words reverberated in his memory. They had come to his rescue, saved him from those vicious women. It was the kid who had stood in the door and tugged him in. Was it the woman who had tended his wounds? He enjoyed the thought.

Travor took a step forward and cleared his throat. The sound was as attention-getting as thunder on a cloudless, sunny day.

Stunned, both people quickly turned to look at him, and paled a little, he thought. The boy dropped the keys and they jangled as they hit the white carpet.

He couldn't begin to understand their reactions. He knew he probably looked a sight. Hell, he hadn't had a haircut in several months, but didn't these people know it was rude to stare? He shifted his stance, uncomfortable. He felt thoroughly exposed. Bare chest. Bare feet. He didn't make a habit of roaming around unclothed in front of women, but there seemed little he could do about it. He hoped her husband didn't pop in.

Neither of them spoke, so Travor took another step toward them. He spoke. "'Scuse me, ma'am. But can someone tell me what's going on?"

Erin jerked at the sound of his voice. The Southern drawl was soft and much too familiar. It seemed to roll all the way from his abdomen and out that sensuous, finely shaped mouth. She looked at her son, who nodded in what seemed to be an I-told-you-so manner.

Max stepped forward. "Sure, mister. You were being mobbed by your fans and my mom and I rescued you."

Travor frowned. "Fans?"

The three of them stared at each other until Travor began to feel like the wart on the end of old Doc Linstrom's nose back home. He looked around the room just so he didn't have to watch them watch him. *Not as bad as the bedroom, but a little overdone in Presley.*

"Ya'll Elvis fans?" Travor asked, nodding toward a wall where a huge portrait of the man hung, then waited for an answer.

Erin's heart fluttered uncontrollably. His voice melted over her. He'd used just the right amount of slur. He had that dazed, vulnerable look that no Elvis impersonator had ever been able to emulate. He was perfect. But Erin wasn't about to answer him. It sounded like a trick question. She had a premonition that a hidden camera was going to pop out of the closet. This has to be a joke, she thought. It just has to be.

Suddenly she whirled toward Max. "Of course," she said, drawing the words out in an I'm-going-to-get-even tone of voice. "Your grandma's behind this, isn't she? She hired this look-alike and staged the scene. That's why she gave us all those coupons for that fast-food joint. And you were in on it, weren't you, Max? You're the one who suggested that restaurant tonight. And it was your idea to rescue him." She took a step toward the kid. "Ha, ha, the joke's on me, right?"

Travor stepped toward the kid, too. "Now, wait a minute, lady. If this is a joke, then it's on me."

Both the woman and the son ignored him.

"Grandma doesn't joke about the King. You know that, Mom."

"What king? What are you people talking about?"

Erin was only vaguely aware of the man's protestations. She tuned him out completely and slumped in the chair, frustrated. Max was right. Lou Weller was a dedicated, devoted fan. She owned every book written about Elvis but she refused to read them. Instead, she forced others to read them to her, demanding they skip over anything that sounded blasphemous, as she put it. She didn't even approve of Elvis impersonators, unless they were good. *Really, really* good.

And this guy looks good, Erin thought. Like the real McCoy. Lou would probably be taken with this one.

Travor stood in the middle of the floor. He felt as though he'd been saved by a couple of cuckoos. Who would have thought it? Mother and son both. But then he'd often heard that sort of thing ran in families. He studied them, unconsciously rubbing his chest.

Erin watched as the large hand, fingers splayed, raced from his chest to his navel and back again. She remembered how warm his skin had been when she'd lifted him from the van. She thought of his arm around her shoulders as they'd made their way toward the house. And how her own fingers had gently medicated his wounds, lingering here and there as if they had a mind of their own. She felt mesmerized by his actions. *So much hair... so thick... so curly...*

Hair! A flood of relief mingled with disappointment flushed through her. "It's not him. I knew it wasn't."

"Not who?" And then it registered. "You're kidding, lady. Tell me you're kidding." Travor stopped. She looked so angry, so disillusioned, he couldn't continue. Her voice was laced with accusation as if he had personally, purposely wronged her. "Are you thinking what I think you're thinking?"

No one answered him.

"Are you sure, Mom?" Max asked.

"Of course, I'm sure. Look at that chest."

Max walked hesitantly toward Travor and leaned close. He studied the curly black hair from navel to throat.

Travor gazed down too, mentally preparing himself for pain in case the kid reached out and plucked.

"Elvis didn't have any chest hair. At least, not that much," the woman said.

I was right. They are nuts. "What the blazes has chest hair got to do with anything?" he asked, but they gave him little more than a cursory glance.

"Just check *Flaming Star* or the *Blue Hawaii* tape. Any of his movies. You'll see." She was confident. Her chin jutted forward.

"The medicine did it." The kid seemed just as confident.

"What medicine?" Travor asked. They'd really thrown him this time. *Medicine?*

"Max, please. If you think the medicine they gave him for that so-called mysterious disease he supposedly had caused all that hair to grow, then you've lost it, kiddo. It would be on the market and every bald head in the world would be swigging it down, or rubbing it on or—"

Travor wanted to laugh. Mom and kid both had some imagination. *Maybe I'll play along... just for the fun of it. See how far they go.* "It's hereditary," Travor interrupted. He got their attention.

Erin and Max stared up at the tall man, mouths open.

"My daddy had a full head of hair up to the day he died. So did Grandpa and I understand his father did, too."

"So did Vernon," Max reminded his mother.

"Who's Vernon?" Travor asked.

"You don't have amnesia, do you?" Max asked, sitting on the arm of his mother's chair.

Travor rubbed the back of his head, conceding that these two were prepared to go the whole nine yards. "Maybe I do or maybe we're all trapped in a nightmare." They didn't crack a smile.

"Do you remember that we brought you to Grandma's house in our van?" Max asked.

I wouldn't have come to this nuthouse on my own, Travor thought. "Vaguely," he answered.

Max queried further. "Do you remember all those women chasing you?"

Travor winced. "I've got the scars to prove it." He glanced at the woman but she looked away. "Ma'am, thanks for rescuing me. I reckon they would have killed me."

Max laughed. "They just wanted a piece of you for their scrapbooks. You ought to see my grandma's scrapbooks."

A piece of me? Travor frowned. *These people are damned serious.* "Look, uh, there's been some kind of mistake here. I'm just a country boy from East Texas who—some say—looks like—"

He stopped. They were staring at him as if he was about to tell them a joke they'd heard many times before. "I guess you've heard the punch line," he mumbled.

"You're going to tell us you're not an Elvis impersonator," Erin stated.

"You got it," he answered.

"You mean you're not Elvis? You haven't been in hiding?" Max asked incredulously.

Travor was stunned. Damn, people had made a fuss over his looks since he'd dropped the weight, but this was downright ridiculous. He studied the mother. From the expression on her face, he could see she didn't think it was ridiculous. She looked like she could get as violent as those parking-lot women. He turned toward the kid. *Obviously his mind was made up.*

Travor cleared his throat, ready to defend himself, but then his own mother's words popped into his head. *When in doubt, don't.* He'd learned that some of her advice was worth taking. "Are you kidding? Elvis Presley?" He smiled for the first time. His eyes crinkled in typical Presley fashion and his lips curved appealingly lopsided.

Erin almost panicked when a light-headedness overtook her and a dizziness followed in its wake. She fought to squelch the pleasant sensation that rippled through her body. She knew what had caused it. That's not a smile. It's a Presley sneer.

The tension had eased somewhat. Introductions had been made, although Travor felt certain the kid still thought he was Presley in the flesh. His mom looked and acted as though a double load of pulpwood had been lifted from her shoulders. But she was acting cool toward Travor and he wondered why. The van had been stashed in the garage; the curtains had been checked for cracks. They were in the kitchen now, trying to conjure up a meal for three out of assorted leftovers.

Travor was drinking a glass of ice water and munching wilted celery stalks stuffed with cream cheese. The kid had insisted on nuking some bacon—charred crunchy—just the way Elvis had liked it. He made a mental note to watch his diet around the kid; it would be easy to blow it if he ate everything Elvis supposedly ate.

"So you decided on Memphis first," Erin said, nibbling on a piece of toasted wheat bread.

"Yeah. Bad choice, considering...but I haven't been out of the East Texas area since I was a boy so I thought I'd bike through Arkansas and on into Memphis. Head home by way of Jackson and New Orleans."

"You've never traveled?" Max asked, incredulously.

"I sure haven't, but that's fixing to change. After I spend a few weeks at home, taking care of business, I'm gonna hit the roads again. There's lots to see out there."

"I've been all over and I'm only eleven."

"Don't brag, Max."

Travor smiled. "When I was eleven I was working in my dad's electrical shop back in East Texas. I had a little fix-it corner where I worked on toasters, and irons and all sorts of things."

"Wow, you made your own money at eleven. See, Mom, he had a job. Why can't I have one?"

Travor interrupted. "No, son, I didn't earn that money for me. That was the family money. We were pretty poor. Even though we owned some land, we barely made ends meet."

Erin peeled some crust from the bread she was holding and nibbled at it. She leaned against the counter, listening. It was hard to imagine a grown man who had never been anywhere. It was even more difficult to imagine Travor Steele as an eleven-year-old boy, helping his family eek out a living. She couldn't help but comment. "Things sure would've been different for you if you'd grown up as Lou's son."

Max nodded in agreement. "You can say that again. Tell him, Mom."

Erin pointed a finger at Max, a warning to control himself. Then she continued. "I can't imagine living in one place all my life. I was born in Tulsa and by the time I was nine months old, I'd been to Louisville, Kentucky, Boulder, Colorado, Houston, Texas, and Mobile, Alabama. That was only the beginning."

"Your father must have been relocated a lot."

Erin laughed. "You could say that. My father worked for Elvis for a while. But my traveling came about after my parents divorced."

"Grandma's really cool. They call her a groupie. She's always been one. She says she's the queen of the groupies."

Erin felt her face going red. "She used to be, Max. She's a lot more settled now." She saw him make a face at Travor and decided to change the subject.

"Too bad your plans have been interrupted. Memphis is an interesting city. So's Jackson. You would have enjoyed spending some time touring them." She noticed that she was saying the words to the floor and berated herself for it. But she was having the darndest time looking at the guy. Every time she did, her heart pumped violent spasms all the way to the tips of her toes.

"But I'm not going to change my plans."

Travor was as stunned as the woman when the words popped out of his mouth. She'd looked at him then, for sure. Her big blue eyes had popped open even wider and she'd almost dropped the slice of bread she held.

He shrugged as she looked at him. "I've got places to go and people to see," he explained. What if he told her that staying in Memphis just might have something to do with the way the ceiling fan made fine white-gold wisps caress the side of her cheek, or the fact that she was ringless. Whatever the reasons, he could tell by the wrenching in his chest that he was definitely attracted to her. Of course, that uncomfortable feeling might be caused by the charred black bacon the kid had made him sample.

"Hey, neato! You're gonna stay? You can have Grandma's room. I can't wait till Grandma gets home. She's gonna freak out." The kid was clearly ecstatic.

His mom wasn't. "He can't stay here!" she said to Max, then turned her attention to Travor. "You can't possibly be serious. You can't tour Memphis. Especially now—in August. This is the anniversary of his death. This is a big deal. Elvis impersonators are all over the place and they don't run when their fans take off after them. That's what got you in trouble. You ran."

"Sorry, but it's a little difficult to stand still and let a bunch of crazed women tear you apart."

Erin frowned. "Look, this is just the wrong month for you to be here. People from all over the world are going to converge on Graceland in two weeks for the annual candlelight vigil. There's no way you can walk down the street.... You ... It's absolutely..."

"C'mon, Mom. Let's keep him till Grandma gets home. She won't care," Max insisted. He turned to Travor. "She always lets people stay over. She discovers stars and singers. She makes records and we're gonna start making videos and—"

"Don't you realize how you look?" Erin interrupted.

Travor was torn between the two. He wanted to ask Max all kinds of questions about his grandmother, as well as his mother. But the woman was staring at him suspiciously.

"I look like Travor Steele from Rattan, Texas. I've looked this way all my life and no one's ever mistaken me for Elvis Presley." It was just a tiny lie, he thought. He didn't look the way he'd always looked, but he pushed that thought away and continued. "You people here in Memphis just have a one-track mind." He wished Erin was just a little glad he planned to stick around. Didn't she feel the tug of attraction?

Max laughed and looked at his mother. "C'mon, Mom. This will be fun. We can dress him up in some of those costumes Grandma made. He'll look awesome! We can even enter him in a look-alike contest. Boy, when Grandma walks through that door she'll—"

"Put a lid on it, Max. He isn't a toy and this isn't a game." She turned her attention toward Travor, focusing her light blue eyes somewhere above his black hair. "Mr. Steele, you won't be able to set foot out this door. Little more than an hour ago, a special news bulletin pronounced Elvis alive and well and somewhere here in Memphis. In case you're a little dense, you look like the real thing—especially to people who have forgotten just what the real thing looked like. Those news bulletins are talking about you."

"That's their mistake—"

"But it's your problem, as well as ours. They showed us rescuing you. I'm surprised they're not pounding on the door by now. I'm surprised the phone isn't ringing off the—" She stopped short. "The phone!"

Quickly Erin left the kitchen.

"Mom's gonna take the phone off the hook so no one can call us. Boy, is Grandma gonna be mad."

"Why?" Travor asked.

"'Cause when Grandma learns you're here, she's gonna try to call us and tell us exactly what to do. That always happens. I'm sure Grandma has real cool plans for you."

Erin returned and stood in the middle of the kitchen. She ran both hands through her shiny gold hair, then picked up her conversation right where she'd left off. "I don't have the slightest idea how to go about getting this matter straightened out."

"Call the TV stations," Max suggested.

"Call the newspapers," Travor added and winked at Max.

Erin wasn't humored. "Why not the fire department or the police? Better yet, the FBI."

"I wish you would call the police and ask about my bike and duffel bag," Travor stated, rubbing the back of his head.

"Wow, a motorbike!" Max exclaimed with envy.

"A brand-new Harley," Travor boasted, but Erin wasn't impressed.

"All my clothes were in that bag, and a tape of—"

"Tape?" she interrupted. "Oh, God, please tell me it was a Dolly Parton tape." She could feel a huge ball form in the pit of her stomach. She gripped the sink tightly.

Travor grinned.

"George Strait?" she squeaked.

Travor shook his head.

"Don't tell me you sing." Her voice was a whisper.

"Okay, I won't—"

"Awesome..." Max interrupted, drawing the word out in admiration.

The ball in Erin's stomach exploded into a thousand little acidic pieces. "Why me, Lord?" she mumbled.

Travor grinned almost shyly, raised his hand and brushed wildly at his already wild hair.

The movement brought a surge of déjà vu.

"Radical!" Max yelled and pointed at Travor. "Regulation haircut, 1958. Remember the documentary, Mom?"

She remembered. The entire world had seen Elvis sitting in the barber's chair, had watched as he'd lifted his right arm, brushed at the spiked regulation haircut, then grinned shyly at the television camera. The scene was one of Lou's favorites.

Erin gulped and grabbed tighter hold of the sink, certain she was going to swoon in typical groupie fashion.

"Mom isn't usually this flaky. I guess she's just upset because they got our license number. She really didn't mean to be rude," Max explained in a grown-up voice that made Travor smile.

"That's okay," Travor answered. But he was disappointed. After they'd talked Erin into letting him stay, he'd hoped the kid would bounce on to bed and he could sit with Erin awhile, get to know her, find out just why his stomach sort of leaped every time he looked at her. He hadn't dated much since he was a teenager, but even the few women he knew had never affected him like this one. The kid hadn't gone to bed; the mom had, leaving strict momlike instructions for them both.

"Max, see that Mr. Steele has whatever he needs. I don't want either of you to fool with the phone, open the door or turn on the television. I don't want to know what the world is doing or thinking. I've had enough."

Now in the overdecorated bedroom, Max was giving the grand tour, pointing to the closet. "Grandma made some clothes just like Elvis wore in concert."

"Why?"

Max shrugged. "I don't know. It's kinda her hobby. She likes flashy stuff. Wait till you see her. She wears an eye patch just for fun, and boy, does she love Elvis!"

Travor looked around the bedroom. "There's no doubt about that, but what about your mom? Does she—is she a groupie, too?"

"No way. Mom owns half of the recording studio and fusses with Grandma about giving all this up. Mom says we need to get normal."

Travor grinned at the kid. "What does your dad say?"

"I don't have a dad. Hey, look at this," Max said, holding up a tube of lipstick. "This is the original 'Love Me Tender' pink. Grandma has it all and—"

Travor didn't want to hear about Grandma and all her treasures. He wanted to pursue the "dad" line of questioning but he wasn't quite sure how to handle it. The kid had changed the subject so fast, Travor wasn't sure if the subject was a touchy one. He decided to use a little child psychology—the kind his friends were always talking about. He put his hand on Max's shoulder.

"I don't have a dad, either, Max. Mine died when I was pretty young and I—"

"Yeah, my dad is dead, too. He was in a bus wreck on the way to marry my mom. My dad played bass guitar for the Roughhousers. Mom says he was the best bass guitar player in the history of rock and roll, and the Roughhousers would've been great someday. They were all killed. A train hit them. Mom always gets real sad when we talk about it. What are you going to sleep in?"

"Well, I—"

"I don't think Grandma has any men's pajamas but when you get up in the morning you can put on some of that other stuff." He grinned. "Wow! You're gonna look radical!"

So much for child psychology, Travor thought, looking down at the small, underweight kid. He decided to mind his own business for a while. "Thanks, Max. Why don't you run along now and get some sleep yourself? You've had quite a night, what with capturing Elvis and making the evening news."

Max grinned. "Yeah, it was the best time I've had. Even better than when me and Grandma slipped through the stage doors to see Garth Brooks. We didn't even get caught because Grandma knows all the tricks. But sometimes I think the guards just let her get away with things 'cause of her age. She's been doing it for a long time."

"Yeah," Travor murmured. "Your grandma sounds like quite a card."

"She is," Max answered proudly. "Just wait till you meet her."

Travor ushered the boy toward the bedroom door. "Oh, I doubt if I get to meet her. Your mother said she had another week left in—"

Max was shaking his head seriously. "Mom's not thinking," he whispered. "When Grandma hears that Elvis is in Memphis, she's gonna be on the first plane home. She flew to Michigan when you were there! I mean—"

Travor winced at Max's faux pas and gently pushed him out the door. "Good night, kid," he said and closed it on Max's, "You're going to meet her. You'll see."

"God forbid," Travor breathed toward the ceiling and was stunned to find it papered in the same manner as the walls. "Granny's got to be a nut!" he swore.

He picked his way through the congested room. Elvis pictures were in ornate frames, everywhere. He

chose one and retreated to the bathroom. Curiously, he
stood in front of the mirror and held the picture beside
his face. Yeah, they looked alike. But he'd known that.
Hadn't his mother always told him if he lost weight he'd
be as handsome as Elvis Presley? But that had been a
joke. Nothing but a joke.

Back home, friends didn't go on about the resem-
blance. But he knew why. In Rattan, Texas, population 700, people knew him as a fat kid. No doubt they
always would because nothing ever changed in Rattan,
Texas. He would always be Dorothy Steele's fat little
boy.

When Dorothy Steele was diagnosed with cancer,
Travor had stayed with her, nursed her through the
horrible disease that eventually took her life. It was
during that time he began to lose weight, exercise, jog.
Then he'd sold the family business, and impulsively invested in a couple of oil ventures his cousin had put together. Miraculously, the money had started rolling in.
Funny how things happened, he thought. He'd done it
all out of frustration and depression. Celeste Fillmore
pushed her way into his mind. Was she a result of his
frustration and depression? He didn't even want to
think about her. It was because of Celeste that he'd decided to leave Rattan, get away... find himself.

And I'm having a damned good time doing it.

Travor left the bathroom and replaced the picture on
the dresser. He roamed cautiously around the room,
and moved toward the closet. Wonder just how many
costumes the old lady made? he mused. He pulled open
the door and stared openmouthed. Bright glittery fab-
rics hung preciously along the rail. Huge ornate belts
dangled from a rack. On the right, tucked next to the
wall, capes flowed to the floor.

He shut the door gently and swore beneath his breath. Erin's mother was obviously more than a die-hard fan. Come to think of it, all these people were so far from dead-center normal, he'd probably better get out of Memphis as soon as he could. He looked around the room once more before he retreated to the living room. He'd sleep on the sofa. Something about Lou's bedroom made him sad.

Chapter Three

Erin stared at the crack of light beaming through the miniblinds. She'd been bug-eyed ever since she'd come to bed, listening for sirens, a pounding at the door. And now it was morning. *Wonder why it's taking them so long to track us down?*

An Elvis sighting always brought publicity. But in August, it seemed worse. During the anniversary month of his death, every major television network was showing his movies or documentaries of his life. Every newspaper ran a feature story; every tabloid made note of a sighting. Even the Disney Channel had been pushing Elvis Presley. There was nothing the media liked better than to hear that the "real" Elvis had been spotted.

Erin tossed the comforter aside and scrambled off the bed. She hadn't changed into her nightgown, not under the circumstances. She'd wanted to be prepared for a quick exit. Too, she didn't want to be wearing her flimsy nightshirt with the stranger in the house. There was too much electricity between them. She frowned, wondering if her imagination was getting the best of her. She didn't remember Max's father affecting her this way. She didn't recall having sweaty palms and heart palpitations. Maybe that was because it was love, she thought. True love. Only puppy love caused sweaty palms and pounding hearts. Besides, she wasn't normally attracted to *anyone* who resembled Elvis Presley. In fact, she steered clear of anyone who had anything to do with the entertainment industry. There was no future in it.

Still, when this Travor Steele looked at her, it wasn't like when Tommy at the Quick-Serve looked at her, and Tommy was every bit as good-looking. When Travor Steele smiled, it had just a hint of flirt in it. He'd even winked a couple of times, making her blood simmer.

"I'm acting like a teenager," she said aloud and stood swiping at her wrinkled shirt. Thoughtfully, she peered through the blinds. The neighborhood looked deserted and lonely. She hummed a couple of notes of "Love Me Tender," then grumbled, disgusted with herself. She didn't even like that dull song, so why was it dancing in her head? She knew why. Travor Steele.

She forced all thoughts of the Texan out of her mind, and allowed her gaze to roam the yard. Suddenly, Mrs. Tillotson ran past the window in her tattered robe and a nightcap. Erin gasped.

She did remember our white van. She definitely saw the newsbreak.

Erin hurried out of her room and to the front door. She was standing on the threshold just as old lady Tillotson tiptoed past.

"Good morning, Mrs. Tillotson," Erin greeted and felt a stab of satisfaction that she'd startled the woman.

"Oh, uh, good morning, Erin. I was just looking for the, uh, morning paper and—"

"Your paper or ours, Mrs. Tillotson?" Erin asked.

"Well, uh, mine, of course. Why would I be looking for yours?"

Erin smiled. "You are in our yard."

Mrs. Tillotson looked around, stunned, as if she had no earthly idea how she'd gotten there.

"I suppose you heard that Elvis is in town." Erin believed in taking the bull by the horns or, in this case, the trespasser by the sleeping cap.

"Why, no . . . I mean . . . is he, now?"

"Yes. He showed up last night at a burger joint right here in Memphis. He has a penchant for hamburgers, you know. Always did. Of course, he couldn't get anywhere near a burger in this town. Someone in a white van rescued him before he was almost decapitated by a mob of fans. Isn't that something?"

"Landsakes . . . a white van . . ." Her eyes darted to the closed garage door.

"You wouldn't be heading for our garage to check out our license plate, now would you?" Erin asked.

The old woman's face turned red. "Why, Erin Weller, how could you ask such a thing? I know how you feel about mingling with superstars. But surely you'd—"

"No, I wouldn't," Erin interrupted. "I wouldn't rescue Spider-Man off flypaper, so you can go on home because Elvis isn't here."

"Well, I never!"

"That makes two of us," Erin whispered and watched the old woman totter toward her own house.

"What was that all about?" a voice behind her asked.

Erin whirled around. The sight before her completely took her breath away. She inhaled several king-size gulps trying to get control of herself.

Travor Steele stood before her, dressed in a familiar, tight-fitting, black leather jumpsuit, slashed open to the waist. His chest hair peeked out, brazenly.

Erin could feel her mouth moving but nothing came from her lips. She clenched her teeth together so hard they hurt. "Who—what—who said you could go through my mother's closets?" she whispered.

Travor rubbed one leather-clad thigh. "Max," he answered simply.

"Max," she repeated. She pushed away from the door and walked toward the kitchen, steering clear of the handsome, barefoot man.

"Hey, don't be mad," Travor said, following her. "It's just a joke. I did it for the kid. You know, he really thought I was Presley there for a while so I thought—"

"You didn't think at all," Erin snapped. She took out the coffee filters and slammed the cupboard door. Mentally, she railed against her son, her mother, Mrs. Tillotson and the striking look-alike who acted as though he'd dropped off a turnip truck.

"I thought a lot about you."

His voice was a low, throaty whisper. *Sexy* was the correct word. She didn't dare turn to look at him. She knew she was blushing; she could feel her face burn. And she was appalled that her body was responding to his voice, his eyes, his very presence.

Fiddling at the countertop, she did unnecessary things to the imaginary drips and invisible stains. She heard a kitchen chair scrape against the floor and held her breath. Her nerves tingled at the sound of his movements. He was sitting. She could feel those teasing, heavy-lidded eyes watching her every move.

The silence between them was overwhelming. Erin seethed and concentrated on the water from the faucet as she filled the coffeepot. She counted the scoops of coffee, and slipped the filter basket into the coffee-maker. She poured the water through the opening, watching carefully as it filled the reservoir. She flipped on the switch, all the while ignoring her racing pulse and the sinfully beautiful man behind her.

Travor studied her petite form, allowing his eyes to caress her from the top of her head to the heels of her bare feet. He could almost feel her beneath the palms of his hands. Warm. Willing. And waiting. He grinned, appreciating this flight of his imagination as well as how her tight jeans cupped her bottom. They hugged her thighs and calves seductively. The blouse she had on was the same one she'd worn last night, tied at the waist now and wildly, provocatively wrinkled.

She slept in it. Didn't trust me. He was amused by the thought. He'd always had the reputation of being a little shy around women, except for that one time. God, what a mistake that had been. He could still feel the humiliation of standing at the altar, waiting . . . waiting. . . . The bride had never shown. Rumor had it that she'd left town with some salesman, but Travor had never known for sure. And he didn't care. He just wanted her out of his mind, his memory. But that was impossible. He would never forget the embarrassment. He twisted the large diamond ring on his pinkie finger. Never again, he thought, then focused on Erin.

He cleared his throat, thoroughly enjoying the effect it had on her. Her blond head swiveled around and a strand of hair slapped against her cheek. Their eyes met, although hers were quick to rise an inch or two above his eyebrows. "Anything I can do to help?" he whispered.

Erin slumped against the counter. She took a deep breath. "Yes, there is something you can do. You can go back to the bedroom and get out of that ridiculous costume." She held up her hand to stop his objections. "I know it was Max's idea. I also know my son. He's as bad as the media. He wants to wring every ounce of excitement he can out of this situation but it's going to backfire. I can almost guarantee it."

"How can it backfire?" he questioned. "There's no one here to see me except you and Max."

"Listen to me. If the media shows up at the door this morning, all we need is for you to be dressed like..." She let her words drift away because the man was shaking his head, leaning forward with his elbows on the table.

"They're not going to show up. I had identification in that duffel bag. A license with my picture on it. And once they hear that tape—" He laughed.

Erin rolled her eyes. "You are just a country boy, aren't you?" She moved toward the coffeepot and attacked an imaginary splatter with a dish towel. "This is the biggest thing to happen in Memphis in years. Sure, we have our look-alikes and our impersonators, but they don't run from the mobs. You ran. You acted like the real thing. So even if they know you're Travor Steele from Rattan, Texas—even with proof in black-and-white or red-and-yellow—they're going to milk this thing dry." She glared at him. "Didn't you learn anything from that mob last night?"

Travor laughed again and the sound swamped through her, caressing every vital organ in her body. Goose bumps popped out on her skin; she wondered if he could hear them coming up. She turned away, unable to look at him any longer. The urge to touch was overpowering. The desire to get close to him, share his body heat, taste him was more than she could bear. The all-consuming *wanting* was completely new to her, and she could only attribute it to a dormant sex life. Damn Kyle Duncan for leaving her, for dying on her when she and Max needed him. Damn him for never affecting her like this.

Elvis Presley had never affected her like this, either. As many times as she'd seen his movies, she'd never been titillated by his grin, his eyes, his voice. She'd never felt anything more than empathy for the man who had no life of his own. So why... why was she reacting like this to Travor Steele, who could easily be mistaken for his twin brother?

Correction, Elvis himself.

The chair once again scraped against the floor. "Look, I know I'm causing a lot of trouble...."

He was moving toward her. She could feel it. The *Jaws* theme song began to pound in her head and she stiffened, as if waiting for the shock of pain, but savoring each suspenseful moment.

"I really didn't plan this thing."

She could feel the heat of his body, and her reactions to it frightened her. She squeezed her eyes shut.

"Will you turn around and look at me?" He put his hands on her shoulders and turned her around.

She opened her eyes, but they wouldn't focus as she stared into the mass of hair covering his chest.

Travor gently massaged her shoulders, then took one finger and tilted her chin up. "I'm sorry. What do you think we should do? How should we handle this? I'll do anything you say."

His words were lost in a sensual cloud of fantasy that floated through her mind. All she could think about was moving closer, pressing against him.

"Erin . . ."

She couldn't answer. The tone of his voice, that all-male scent dulled her reactions, held her captive in a foggy, hypnotic state.

She didn't even flinch when she saw his mouth coming closer to hers. Such a sexy mouth. So well-defined, and full and—

The soft brush of his lips confirmed everything her body was feeling. His breath against her cheek, her ear, then moving down her neck was as hot as molten lava. She could feel his hands cupping her bottom, squeezing . . . lifting.

"God, you're as hot as you look, and you taste good enough to eat."

His voice was a husky whisper against her heated flesh.

"I was awake all night thinking about this."

Erin held her breath, afraid to move. Afraid he would go further. Afraid he would quit. His hands were moving up her shirt and the heat of them on her skin zapped her all the way to her brain. She thought she could hear his heart beat, or was it hers? Dear Lord, she didn't want to fight the tangle of feelings pulsing through her. She couldn't.

It took everything within her to pull away from him, but she did. Without looking at him, she turned away, inhaled deeply and moved toward the coffeepot.

Be cool, girl. Hang on to your head.

Miraculously, she poured two cups of coffee. She handed one to Travor and was certain he noticed her shaking hand. She clutched her own steaming mug, wrapped ten fingers around it, and looked into his eyes. She couldn't let him know how he'd affected her.

He wasn't smiling. He looked almost as uncomfortable as she felt when he backed away from her. *Good. That would teach him to come on to her.*

She glanced at him again and almost giggled hysterically when she saw the face on Travor's mug, an exact replica of his own. She was losing it. Maybe she'd better lock herself in her room or, better yet, leave the house.

Yeah, that would be better. Leave the house.

She was searching for an excuse to get out of there when the slamming of the front door saved her from the impossible task of thinking straight.

"Hi, Mom. Hey, Travor. Peter's here from across the street. We'll be in my room."

Erin stiffened as her son and the neighbor's boy walked past the kitchen door, looking in at them with ill-disguised interest.

"I thought he was still asleep," Travor said.

Erin shot him a weary look. "So did I, but I should have known better. He's Lou Weller's grandchild and no telling what he's up to."

Lou Weller? It was the first time Lou's last name had been mentioned, and it reminded Travor of what the kid had told him last night. Max had never known his father. He told himself to tread lightly; the woman might be looking for a father for her son. Before he could think another thought, Max and Peter walked past the door again, glanced at Travor, then left the house.

Travor sat back down at the kitchen table. "See there. The kid didn't think anything of my appearance. I wonder where he's from. Certainly not Memphis."

Erin rolled her eyes and thought once again about the turnip truck. Before she could respond the front door opened a second time. Max and a blond-haired youth Erin had never seen before walked past, looking in, curiously.

Travor was about to speak but Erin held up her hand, silencing him. A few seconds later, the two kids left the house.

The third time it happened, Erin was ready. Max was ushering another stranger through the living room when his mother met him in the hall. She grabbed him by the collar. "Okay, how much have you made so far?" she asked. Her voice had taken on that momlike tone Travor had heard the night before, and he strained his ears to hear what Max would say.

"Nine dollars," Max mumbled, somewhat sheepishly, Travor thought. He grinned. *So the kid's making money off me. Sharp kid.* He felt an enormous amount of pride in the boy, even if his mother didn't.

"Six," the other young voice spouted. "I ain't seen nothing so you gotta give my money back."

Uh-oh. Dissatisfied customer, Travor thought. He pushed away from the kitchen table, walked to the door and presented himself.

"Wow!" the long-haired boy exclaimed, paled, and ran toward the front door.

Max laughed. "Did you see that, Mom? He got his money's worth, for sure. Thanks, Travor!"

Travor winked at Max, then turned an innocent expression toward Erin, who was frowning her disapproval.

"Smart move," she growled. "This is all we need. It's not enough they have our license-plate number." She shook Max's shirt collar roughly. "You *have* to go rounding up customers for show-and-tell. Where the heck are you finding these people at—" she looked at her watch "—eight-fifteen in the morning?"

Max looked surprised. "Gee, Mom, go look out the window."

The lawn was freckled with people, among them, Mrs. Tillotson from next door. She wore a wide-brimmed straw hat and pedal-pushers, and wove through the sparse crowd.

Erin groaned.

Travor gulped.

Max grinned from ear to ear. "I thought you knew they were out there, Mom."

She glared at her son. "How could I know? I've been playing hostess to the superstar, here." She jerked her head toward Travor, who was still peeking through the drapes. "Get away from that window!" she ordered.

Travor jumped at her harshness and stepped back.

"Boy, you really look—"

"I know," Travor interrupted Max. "Awesome."

"Radical!" Max corrected.

"Ridiculous," Erin supplied. But he didn't look ridiculous. He looked downright edible. He was the most beautiful man she'd ever seen, and she suspected he knew it. "One glimpse of you in that black leather and they'll be beating down our door," she murmured in a low husky voice.

Travor and Max looked at each other, confused by her contradiction as well as the tone she'd used. They crossed the floor silently, hesitantly. Travor took a seat right beneath the Elvis portrait. Max sat at his feet.

"What should we do?" Travor asked. "I really didn't believe it when you said you expected this sort of thing."

Erin pierced him with pale blue eyes, and gave a derisive snort. "Believe me, I'm not the dramatic type. I don't cry wolf unless there is a wolf." She turned her attention toward Max. "Where did those people come from? Are you responsible for rounding them up?"

Max shook his head. "Most of them live on this street, Mom. Peter said they all saw the news last night and recognized me in our van. He wanted to come over right then but his mom wouldn't let him. She said there was going to be another raid over at that crazy Weller house."

"Humph!" Erin said and rubbed the bridge of her nose.

"Should we call the police?" Travor asked. "I feel guilty for causing so much trouble, but who would have thought that—"

"Just let me think," Erin interrupted. She crossed the room and threw herself into the bucket chair. *Thank God I uplugged the telephones last night. What else should I do? What would Lou do in situation like this?* But she knew what Lou would do; milk it for everything she could get out of it.

They sat quietly. Travor watched her think. She rubbed her temple, brushed at her hair. He hoped to God she came up with a solution soon. The leather jumpsuit was hot. In spite of the air-conditioning, he was perspiring. How the hell did the man ever perform in black leather? Especially under all those lights? Travor wondered. He tugged at the waist, blew his breath across his chest.

Max was fidgeting on the floor.

Travor saw the front door ease open quietly and a white-gold head pop through. The elflike face, adorned with a black leather patch over one eye, turned toward him. A body followed, along with an eerie, nerve-damaging scream. The body slumped to the floor.

"Grandma!" Max yelled.

"Oh, my God!" Erin breathed.

"What the—" Travor stood and watched as the two of them ran to the prostrate form.

"She's had a heart attack!" Max predicted. Then a crowd of people were pushing their way through the entrance paying little attention to the unconscious woman stretched before them.

"There he is!"

"Get him, get him!"

"Elvis . . . It's really Elvis!"

Travor had the feeling he was caught up in an old horror film that someone had colorized. The small mob coming toward him was as psychedelic as the fear resounding through his veins. Total chaos surrounded him, making it next to impossible to hear Erin's voice.

"Run! Travor, run!"

He hesitated.

"To the bedroom!" she screamed.

He broke to the left, knocking over a lamp as he dodged a short, chubby woman in rainbow-colored leggings. He careened around the doorway and through the hall. Muffled footsteps on the carpet told him he was being pursued.

He made it to the bedroom and slammed the door, thankful there was a lock. He pressed his cheek against the cool wood and gasped for breath. His heart was pounding.

The door vibrated against the brutal attack of so-called friends and neighbors. Travor moved away from it. He felt angry.

This has gotten out of hand. Things have gone too far. He took a deep, deep breath, and then another. Rolling his shoulders, he willed himself to relax, then moved toward the door. He was going to settle this matter once and for all.

Chapter Four

Erin's heart pounded against her chest as she and Max lifted Lou from the floor and helped her to the sofa. This was too much: the screaming crowd, her mother fainting. In her mind's eye, Erin could see a replay of that horrible day at the Astrodome in Houston, Texas. But Lou hadn't fainted then. She'd simply lost her balance, fallen and had been trampled by the fans. Lou had been badly injured—three cracked ribs and a broken collarbone. Erin shuddered at the memory. It had been a frightening experience for her, a horrible thing to witness. Of course, Lou used the experience to her advantage, donning glittery eye-patches to commemorate the near tragedy.

"You okay, Grandma?" Max was fanning the woman vigorously with a magazine.

Lou patted his cheek. "I'm okay, baby. But who is that guy?" She turned to Erin. "Have you questioned him? Has he told you anything?"

Erin frowned. She could feel Lou's excitement and it angered her. "I know who he isn't." Her voice was harsher than she'd intended, laden with disapproval. She corrected it. "Are you really okay? Why did you faint?"

Lou placed her hand over her heart. "It was just like old times. I felt I had to..." she whispered.

"You mean you did that on purpose? How could you scare us that way? You oughta—" A noise from the hall interrupted her. The crowd was getting violent; they shouted, pounded on the bedroom door.

"We gotta help him, Mom," Max said.

An uncontrollable shiver raced down her spine. She wanted to help him but she wasn't about to confront that mob. Her fear of crowds went deep. If she hadn't been within the confines of her van the night before, she'd never have intervened on Travor's behalf. She shook her head. "He's on his own. Besides, there's nothing we can do. If he's smart, he'll go out the bedroom window and run as fast as he can all the way back to East Texas."

"Texas? Is that where he's from?" Lou questioned. "What brought him here? Has he got an act together?"

Erin shuddered. "An act?"

Lou made an impatient sound. "Didn't you look at him? No one looks like he does by accident. He came to see me. He's out to make a name for himself."

It had never dawned on Erin that Travor Steele might be trying to get discovered. She felt like a fool. She didn't want him to be another impersonator. She wanted him to be exactly what he said he was. Subconsciously, she had refused to accept the most logical explanation. Yes, it made sense. It made a lot of sense. She smirked. "He's got an act, all right."

A door banging against a wall interrupted her angry thoughts.

"Get back! I don't want to hurt anyone. I don't want to get hurt, either."

The swarm of people emerged, pressed together. They backed through the hall doorway, stepping on each other's toes.

Then Travor appeared, holding Lou's old Washburn guitar by the neck and using it like a poker.

Erin's heart pounded a little harder. His hair was askew; perspiration streamed down his face, disappearing in his sideburns. The black leather top of the jumpsuit gaped. She wouldn't have been surprised to hear heraldic horns, the drumbeat of *Thus Spake Zarathustra*, the theme music from *2001*. He looked as though he'd been in concert.

The small crowd was obviously taken by his appearance, too. They silently stared at him, starting with his feet and working their way up. They whispered, mumbled, oohed and ahed. Erin half expected them to leap at any moment, grab handfuls of black leather, black hair... flesh.

Travor didn't wait for them to act. "You should be ashamed of yourselves. What kind of friends are you?" he asked. He pointed the guitar at Lou. "You've invaded this lady's home, almost trampling her."

"Great guns, girl, that boy can act!" Lou whispered.

Erin grinned in spite of herself. "It's the Presley charm, remember? He's got it down pat."

"You've trespassed and I think you owe the whole family an apology."

Erin, Lou and Max stared at the crowd; the crowd stared back. They didn't look very apologetic, Erin noted.

They weren't.

"I think you owe us!" Mrs. Tillotson stepped forward haughtily.

"Me?" Travor asked. Surprised by the turned tables, he gripped the guitar tighter and looked at Erin questioningly. His innocent expression tugged at her heart.

"Yeah, you owe us. We want to know why you skipped out and played dead. How could you do it to us?"

Obviously, a number of people agreed with Mrs. Tillotson. They became noisy in their demands; they were getting angry.

"Do you realize how long we stood in line just to view your body? And now we know for certain it wasn't even you."

Travor tried to say something but their voices drowned out his explanations.

"All that mourning . . . all that crying . . . You don't know the pain you caused—" Mrs. Tillotson was getting dramatic.

"Not to mention going out and spending fortunes for those last souvenirs," a man complained.

They pressed toward him but Travor waved the guitar. He poked and prodded them toward the front door.

"I am not Elvis Presley!" he shouted.

They were stunned into silence and glared at him as if he'd pulled a cruel trick.

He softened his voice. "I know how badly you want to believe he's still alive but I swear, I'm not him."

They didn't answer. He could tell by their faces that they doubted every word he said. He ran his left hand through his hair. "I don't know how to get through to you people."

He looked so helpless, Erin wanted to run to him, protect him from the fans who wanted nothing more than a tangible piece of him. She stifled the urge, telling herself he'd asked for it.

"Look at me. Think about it. Use some sense! I'm thirty-one years old."

In spite of her own resentment and suspicions, Erin cheered him on. Surely they would come to their senses now.

"How old would Elvis be today?" Travor asked.

"Good question," Erin whispered.

Lou shook her head and muttered, "Nice try, but it won't work. We don't care what Elvis would look like today. We'll always remember him the way he was."

Erin frowned, realizing her mother was right.

"Don't try to con us!" a woman shrieked. "You haven't changed a bit."

Travor shook his head, took a deep breath. He didn't know what to do next. This crowd had tunnel vision. Then he remembered Erin's argument to Max. He pulled at the leather jumpsuit. "Look! I've got hair on my chest."

Everyone stared; they didn't understand.

"Elvis didn't. Check the...the, uh—" He glanced at Erin helplessly. "Check that Hawaii tape...any of his movies...you'll see."

"That can be faked!"

"You could have shaved your chest for the movies!"

Travor realized with a sinking feeling they didn't care that he was too young, too hairy. It was hopeless. They wanted their King and they wanted him now.

He waved the guitar. "Okay, I'll give you what you want."

Erin froze, searching his face anxiously for the meaning behind his words. His firm mouth curled as he cleared his throat and paced the floor. His bare feet sank into the plush white carpet. Erin liked the way his body moved, so sensually casual. But she had a feeling she wasn't going to like what he was about to say.

"I'll give you an explanation," he said, stopping short, just inches away from Mrs. Tillotson. He stared straight into her faded blue eyes. He seemed to re-adjust his facial muscles; his eyes hardened. He rolled his shoulders. His body tensed. "Look what you're doing. Same thing. Same as it was before I—I went away. I never had any peace and quiet."

Erin gasped.

Lou sighed.

The crowd gave a collective moan.

The texture of his voice was huskier, softer. His words slurred in a pronounced Elvis-like tone. The transfor-mation took everyone by surprise.

"I couldn't even walk in my own yard without you people trying to—uh—scale my fence."

"But you loved your fans," Mrs. Tillotson argued.

"Yeah, I did till you started to harass me.... I couldn't take it anymore."

"How?" a man asked.

Travor never blinked. "The witness-protection pro-gram."

Erin sat wide-eyed, rigid. "You were right. He is an impersonator, and he's just made a name for himself."

She felt a lump build in her throat and she tried hard to swallow it.

Lou sighed again. "He's good. Oh, boy, is he good. He knows exactly what he's doing."

"This is awesome," Max breathed. He was huddled beside his grandmother on the sofa.

The three of them watched as each person became human again before their eyes. Mrs. Tillotson seemed to slump in defeat. The others shuffled and fidgeted with embarrassment.

Travor jerked the guitar toward the door and they followed his silent order, leaving the house without so much as an apology. He slammed the door behind them.

Erin let out a breath. "He won't be able to leave this house. He's dug his grave, jumped in and pulled the dirt in after him," she murmured.

"Don't worry. I'll dig him out," Lou answered.

Erin frowned. "Don't count on it. This is going to snowball, and we don't have the money to invest in—"

"That's exactly what I want it to do. Snowball."

Erin jerked her head toward her mother. "Leave it alone, Lou. Don't get involved. You remember what happened last time you started working on an Elvis project. We can't afford this."

Their eyes met. "This time will be different. He's exactly what I've been looking for."

"We don't have the funds, Lou."

"We'll find the money somehow. We have to." Lou rubbed her hands together. "This time will be different," she repeated. "I can feel it."

Erin shook her head, fighting the ominous feeling that raced through her. "Please. Don't make it any worse."

Lou ignored Erin's plea and eyed Travor, who was leaning against the locked door. "I'm prepared to go all the way," she mused. "Whatever it takes." Then she turned toward Erin and raised her eye patch. "This is my last chance," she whispered. "I realize that."

Their eyes locked, and Erin knew that she had to support her mother in whatever she wanted to do. If Lou could admit that this time would be the last, that they couldn't afford any more mistakes, then it would be different, Erin thought.

"There's a camera crew out there," Travor interrupted them.

Erin jumped from the sofa and walked quickly to the window. She saw Mrs. Tillotson racing across the yard toward a young reporter who was wielding a microphone. "You've certainly done it now," Erin chastised, and threw a disapproving look at Travor.

He shrugged and ran a hand through his thick, damp hair. He let out a breath and turned away from her. "I don't see as I had much choice." He propped the guitar against the bucket chair, then sank into it himself. He needed some peace and quiet. The coffee seemed to roll in his stomach. He felt sick.

"You acted like you really are Elvis. There's gonna be worldwide hysteria," Max predicted. The boy dropped to the floor beside Travor's chair and laid the guitar across his lap. He stared up in awe at Travor.

Travor glanced at the kid, then closed his eyes. He was tired of people looking at him that way. He wished he could block the past day out of his mind, forget about Elvis Presley, Memphis and the Weller family. They were causing him to make a fool of himself. If anyone back home got wind of this...

He felt someone beside him. He opened his eyes and stared into a piercing blue one and a black patch. So this is Lou Weller.

"You're wrong, you know."

Travor prepared himself. "Wrong about what?"

"The fans. And Elvis. He loved them. He thrived on them and he was good to them."

Travor closed his eyes again. "Sorry. I didn't mean to misrepresent the man. All I know about him wouldn't even fill a pea hull."

"Oh, yeah? Then how did you know he had a fence around his house?" Erin challenged. She was standing across the room but her voice was accusing, hostile.

Travor looked at her. "That's a silly question. A man with a following like his would have to have a fence. Anyway, I was just grasping for something—anything—that would get them out of here."

He could tell Erin wasn't buying it, but he was beyond caring. He checked Lou's reaction and saw a funny little grin quivering on her elflike face.

"I'm Lou," she said.

He couldn't help but smile back. "Yeah, I know." He wasn't certain how this particular fan would react to him but he suspected she would consume him with all the ardor of a true-blue, hard-core Elvisite. He knew he had to be sharp to deal with Lou Weller, and he didn't feel sharp at this particular moment. He was tired, mentally drained. He closed his eyes again.

Lou laughed deep in her throat. Through half-closed eyes, he peered at her standing over him. So much for Max's old granny who was given special privileges because of her age. This pretty lady could pass for Erin's twin, although there was something about her that Erin lacked: a boldness or was it brazenness? There again, it could have been confidence, self-assurance that she was the mistress of her own fate. But it might be the eye patch that gave her that particular look, he thought. She was small, like Erin, with cropped-short hair and triple-pierced ears. Surprisingly, she wore very little makeup. One thing was very evident. *She definitely has plans for me.* He half expected her to rub her hands together and smack her lips.

He saw Erin move toward him, protectively, he thought. Or was that what he wanted to think? She said nothing. Max was still on the floor, still staring.

Lou broke the silence. "Let's turn on the tube. See what we're up against." She picked up the remote control and aimed it at the television. She didn't budge from Travor's side as she flicked from channel to channel. "Max, do we have a blank tape? I want everything recorded."

Travor watched the kid hustle toward the television and punch in a tape.

Erin moved in close. "He has a motorcycle somewhere with his duffel bag of clothes. It might still be at that restaurant or the police could have it by now."

"I'll find it," Lou said, never averting her eyes from the television.

Erin gave Travor an accusing look before she continued. "He sings..." she began.

Lou's head jerked toward him. Her expression was priceless. He thought she paled somewhat but she quickly gained control of her naked emotions. Travor grinned. If only they could hear that tape. He wouldn't bother to explain. Not at this point. They wouldn't listen to him and they certainly wouldn't believe him.

He closed his eyes again and mentally forced himself back home to the peaceful surroundings he'd grown up in. The way he figured it, he had a choice. He could nip this thing now, walk out that door and through the crowd with only minor scrapes and bruises. Or he could hang around, play their game and see what the future would bring. Erin's soft husky voice washed over him as she spoke to her mother, and he remembered how he'd teasingly kissed her not much more than an hour ago. Damn, she'd tasted good.

He made his decision. What did he have to lose?

Erin turned off the shower and stepped out, grabbing a towel and wrapping it around her lithe body. Uneasily, she wondered what Travor was doing. Was he still in front of the TV or peering out the window at the Elvis fans? She grimaced. Her mother and Max had left to check on Travor's cycle and duffel bag. Hopefully, that was all they would do. Erin knew just how much her mother was capable of accomplishing in the space of an hour. While Erin was thoughtful, careful and hesitant in each business decision she made, Lou was just the opposite. With Lou, it was full speed ahead and work out the details later. It wasn't that her ideas were bad; it was just that she didn't take the time to perfect them, make them foolproof. She moved too fast because she was too anxious.

Surely she wouldn't do anything foolish, like set up some interviews between Travor and the media. Erin had pulled Max aside, told him to keep a close eye on his grandma, not to let her do anything crazy, and to try to keep her away from the bank.

As if Max would stop her. He thought his grandma was the greatest thing since Gummy Worms.

Her thoughts turned back to Travor Steele. Why didn't I see it? Erin wondered. Why didn't I suspect he was someone looking to be discovered? She answered her own mental question. You were too attracted to him, fool. You were too busy analyzing every little tingle he caused and you let him do a number on you.

No, I didn't! her mind screamed. He hasn't done a number on me.

There had always been would-be stars in and out of the Weller house and studio. And not a few Elvis impersonators. Of course, none of them looked like Travor Steele. They were too short, too tall, too thin or too fat, yet they all had one thing in common: a fascination with Elvis Presley. And Lou had used each and every one of them to some degree. For commercials, jingles, private parties, grand openings. Not one of them had been what Lou was looking for to accomplish that ultimate dream, but she'd used those wannabes just the same.

No, she hadn't used them. She'd helped them. Wasn't that how she explained it? She'd aided them in accomplishing their dreams.

And speaking of wannabes with dreams... "Oh, God, I completely forgot..."

Erin grabbed the telephone and plugged it in. She punched in the number of the studio. "BeeCee, I'm going to ask you to do something very unpleasant." Erin laughed. "You're absolutely right...call Kimbie Love. I'm not able to keep our appointment today. Would you try to reschedule? Thanks, BeeCee, and believe me, I owe you."

I owe you big time, she thought, remembering Kimbie Love's ugly temper. The young woman had talent if they could just channel it in the right direction. So far, none of them knew exactly which direction. Erin was certain it was Kimbie's vile personality that was confusing them. If she'd calm down, not be so hateful, they maybe could find the right way to promote her. Erin was beginning to think they should never have offered her a contract.

But one never knows. She shrugged, slipping into a pair of loose shorts and a summer blouse. As Lou pointed out, Kimbie Love was different, and she just might prove to be what Star Music Studio needed.

And as Lou also pointed out, Travor Steele was different. But Erin had known it. Still, for the life of her, she couldn't figure out *why* he was different.

Or why he's lying ... And he is lying, she thought.

It was the living room scene that proved it. He'd shifted into his Elvis role with such ease, Erin was certain he'd done it many times. He's definitely an Elvis impersonator, so why wouldn't he admit it?

Just a country boy from East Texas. That sounded good to her. Why couldn't it be true? she wondered. She didn't examine the why of her wants too carefully as she eyed the telephone once again. *Maybe I can find out more about him.*

She grabbed the phone, and quickly punched some numbers. "Information, please, in Rattan, Texas."

It didn't take long for Erin to have a number listed for a Travor Steele. But was he one and the same? She dialed. Area code 903. Nine eight four ...

"Hello," a woman's voice answered.

Erin was stunned. *Is he married?* "Hello, I'd like to talk with Travor Steele, please." She could hear a commotion in the background. Dogs were barking.

"Hang on a minute. Them dogs are after that new cat that showed up yesterday," the woman said, as if Erin knew exactly what she was talking about. A shooing and fussing, then the slamming of a door reached Erin's ears. The woman returned.

"Travor ain't here. Been away a good while now. Can I take a message?"

"Are you...is he..." She couldn't think of a polite way to ask who the woman was but she found she didn't need to.

"I'm Nellie from across the pasture. I'm just checking on this house and feeding all his critters till he gets back. Crazy man. Taking off like that on his motorcycle."

He was the same man!

"He's gonna get hisself killed. His mother wouldn't approve of his gallivanting around like that or the way he's been acting."

Erin decided to take advantage of the woman's openness. "Why not?"

"Why, Dorothy Steele, God rest her soul, was as fine a Christian woman as I ever seen put on this earth. She didn't believe in tempting the devil by making use of the world's playthings. She'd not allowed a motorcycle for sure, and no televisions, either. Travor's just gone off the deep end. Buying that loud thing, and buying that huge TV. Makes me feel like I'm sitting in a walk-in movie. God willing, Travor's gonna snap out of this. I've given it some thought, and reckon it's that midlife crisis Oprah's been talking about."

Erin couldn't help but smile. If Travor Steele was going through a midlife crisis, he certainly didn't look it. "Perhaps you're right. I've seen things like that happen to the best of men. When is Mr. Steele expected back?" she asked.

"Told me he'd see me when he saw me. Now ain't that a lick? He's gotten downright irresponsible ever since he invested in them oil wells. Pays little mind to his country roots anymore. 'Course, I've given it some thought, and I suspect his looks has lots to do with it.''

Erin's heart began to pound. "His looks?"

"Yes'm, he thinks he's really something now that he's gotten on that health kick. Used to eat ever' meal over at Herm's Chicken Hut but now he won't eat anything fried. Told Herm if he'd bake it, Travor'd eat it, but Herm says he can't afford to change up his way of doin' things just to feed Travor. The boy's gotten pretty up-pity, if you ask us. And he runs by my house ever' morning and ever' afternoon with them shorts on and that bright yeller shirt that shows his armpits. He never used to dress thataway. I swear, Dorothy's probably just a-rolling in her grave."

Erin stifled a laugh. It wouldn't do to alienate Nellie. Obviously, the neighbors and the townspeople were watching Travor closely, appalled at his change of habits. "Mrs., uh... Nellie, can you tell me what Mr. Steele looks like? Would he...would you say he resembles...Elvis Presley?"

The cackle at the other end of the line was so loud Erin held the phone away from her ear. Then there was silence and a mumbling sound. Erin could visualize a tiny birdlike woman wiping her eyes with the corner of her apron. "Land sakes, Elvis Presley. I knew that boy looked like someone."

"Then he does look like Elvis."

A squawk answered her, and Erin wasn't sure it was human. Finally, the woman answered. "Travor was sure taken with little Celeste Fillmore that stayed with the Marples over on Cherokee Ridge. Without the Lord's intervention, she never would have taken up with that insurance salesman. Or did he sell pots and pans? Anyway, Celeste planned out this humongous wedding, invited the entire town, then she didn't even show up. Praise God! That was when she worked at Herm's Chicken Hut. Travor'd go in ever' evening after work and they'd talk and visit. Courted for more'n a year, I'd say. 'Course ever'one knew she was just playing him for a sucker. He was beginnin' to get rich, so he'd give her real nice gifts. Then he bought her the biggest ring the town had ever seen. Didn't get that rock in Rattan, that's for sure.''

Erin didn't want to hear about Celeste Fillmore. She felt outraged at Travor, and for him. She was even angrier at Celeste for embarrassing him in front of the whole town. Just who did she think she was, anyway?

"Hmm," Nellie was saying into the phone. "Elvis Presley. I never noticed it before, but now that you mention it... I'll bet it was all them pounds he lost. We never seen him looking so skinny... Hmm, he was a big one. All his life he was a big one."

"Pounds?" Erin asked. "He's lost a lot of weight?"

Suddenly, Nellie became suspicious, as if realizing for the first time that she was talking to a stranger. "Say, who is this? I've heard tell of people who call on the phone to see if a body's home and if they ain't, then their house gets robbed."

"No—I—" Erin began but Nellie interrupted her.

"Well, I just give it some thought and I reckon I'll call up Sheriff Barnes right now and he'll be keeping an eyeball on Travor's place and you can be sure he won't—"

Erin replaced the phone gently in its cradle before she unplugged it. She felt as though that Nellie woman knew exactly who and where she was. Her pulse beat rapidly. So Travor Steele *was* just a country boy who happened to look like Elvis Presley. She shivered and rubbed her arms, roughly. For some reason, she felt he was much, much more than that.

The lawn was packed with people from the media and scores of Elvis fans. Travor was watching the local station; he had a perfect view of Lou's ranch-style house and what was going on just outside the door. He felt like a hostage.

Lou and Max had left more than an hour earlier; where to, they didn't say. Lou had instructed him not to open the door to anyone, not to answer the phone and then had complained briefly that it was odd the phone wasn't ringing. She'd scratched her head and ordered Travor not to give any interviews, period.

As if I would.

Erin had disappeared to the back of the house. He wished she'd hung around, talked to him. He had a lot of questions to ask. Like what he could expect from Lou Weller. And how long the media would be camped on the front lawn. Lou had plans and Travor felt certain they were going to be pretty exotic plans. He was beginning to wonder just what he'd walked into and why he was staying. Was Erin the reason he was willing to make a fool of himself? Hell, no, he wasn't willing to make a fool of himself for anyone. Well, did he honestly enjoy this nonsense? He didn't have an answer for that question, either. Damn, he thought. Having a dull childhood sure could do its damage.

Absorbed in his thoughts, he eased out of the chair and stretched across the floor. He positioned his hands and lifted himself. Push-ups always helped him think more clearly. So did jogging but that was definitely out of the question. He wondered what was happening back in Rattan. Until now, he hadn't really missed being home. Was Nellie taking care of the dogs? Was Doc looking forward to getting the tape Travor was preparing? He continued to lift himself, up and down, up and down, up and down. The tight black leather pulled across his back but he didn't let it hinder his movements. Up and down, up and down, ten . . . eleven . . .

Erin watched as the leather pulled thin across his broad shoulders. She absorbed the muffled sound of his voice as he counted and found herself mentally saying the numbers with him. Her eyes roamed freely down his spine, across his buttocks and the length of his legs.

"He was a big one," Nellie had said.

Hard to believe, she thought. There didn't seem to be an ounce of fat on him, and the night before, when he'd been shirtless, he'd looked delicious.

Erin had witnessed men doing push-ups before and their bulging muscles and slick, sweaty skin never affected her in quite this way. In fact, no one had affected her like this.

The erotic movements of the leather-clad body before her, lifting, then meeting the floor, sent lapping waves of hunger splashing through her.

"One hundred," he breathed and rested.

Erin snapped out of her reverie and walked quickly past him to the sofa. She wished now she'd put on jeans instead of shorts. She could feel his eyes on her. She decided to ignore him, but found she couldn't ignore the tingling sensations that wafted up her legs and spread like wildfire.

"Hi," Travor said, pushing up from the floor and moving to a chair. He was slightly out of breath, perspiring and the black leather was sticking to his skin.

He felt annoyed when Erin didn't answer, but he could play her game. And he would play it, as soon as he figured out what it was.

He eyed her yellow sandals and her slim ankles. His gaze moved slowly up her legs, across her torso to her shoulders and neck. She was tense. Didn't the woman ever relax?

She stared at the television. Travor stared at her. She didn't appear to be interested in conversation. *Tough,* he thought. *I am.*

"All your predictions have come true. What do you think will happen next?"

She frowned at the picture on the television screen. The three youngsters Max had paraded through the house were being interviewed, reminding Erin of the predicament they were in. She turned toward Travor and waved a hand at the screen. "I predict the next time your fans barge through that door, they'll tear you to shreds."

Travor shifted uncomfortably in his chair. "Thanks. I like to know what I have to look forward to." He was a little stunned by her hostility.

Erin, too, was shocked at her tone of voice. Why was she so angry? she wondered. A picture flashed in her mind's eye: Travor, sitting in a fast-food chicken joint, holding a diamond ring toward some bleached blonde wearing tons of makeup. She wiggled on the sofa, and felt irritated by her irrational jealousy. She also felt irritated by Travor's good looks, and Lou's plan to capitalize on them. In fact, she thought, I'm irritated by the entire situation. Not to mention that Nellie woman. Why did she have to tell me his life story?

"I made things worse, didn't I?"

His soft, sexy drawl interrupted her thoughts, but she knew he was referring to how he'd responded to the crowd earlier.

"I suspect you knew what you were doing. You got what you wanted."

Travor looked confused, then ran a hand through his hair. "All I wanted was for them to leave. I don't know why I did it. It just happened. It seemed to...to pop out of my mouth."

Erin grunted in a very unladylike way and glared at him.

"You don't like me, do you?" he challenged. "Or is it Elvis you don't like? I haven't quite figured it out."

She felt her face burn. Obviously, the guy hadn't picked up on her attraction to him. Good. She didn't need to get hung up on a man who looked like Elvis Presley. There would never be any peace in their lives. They would be forever producing Elvis trinkets, posters, key chains or...

She realized he was watching her so she shifted on the sofa to face him.

"I want to know what your game is," she said, conveniently changing the subject.

"My game?"

His innocent, naive expression riled her. "Look, you've fooled a lot of people but you haven't fooled me. You're too good. You're too perfect. Every movement, every nuance is just too Elvis-like. Now what do you want?"

Travor got up from the chair and walked toward her. "A scam, huh? You're pretty sharp."

Erin sat straighter on the sofa. She felt a little uncomfortable with her accusations now. He looked so big moving toward her, peering down at her. She swallowed. "Let's just say I'm . . . rather astute. I haven't been blinded by the stars." She wanted to tell him she knew about his weight problem, and that she knew how hard he'd worked to achieve the Elvis look, but she didn't. She didn't want him to know she'd phoned his home, talked to that Nellie woman.

He'll tell me. If he's really on the level, he'll tell me everything.

Travor rubbed his chin, studying her intensely.

Erin squirmed. "Look, it was pretty obvious," she tried to explain. "I mean, you buzz into Memphis, particularly at this time of year, totally unaware that you look like Elvis Presley? Give me a break, mister. Lou and I have worked with Elvis impersonators. Most of them have to dye their hair and wear makeup to achieve the effect that comes natural to you—"

"So you think I'm after something. Is that it?"

Again she felt a warning pulsing in her head. "Well, sure, it makes sense. You probably heard about Lou or read about her. She was pretty well-known at one time. In fact, they did a profile on her in *Special Reports* a few months ago. Lou has helped lots of would-be singers."

He shook his head. "Sorry. Never heard of her."

"Look, Mr. Steele. It's no crime to want to be somebody, to be discovered. I just don't like the way you went about it." When he started to speak, she put up her hand to stop him. "We've seen everything. People will go to any length to get their names in lights, but I personally detest tricks, schemes and devious plotting, so—"

He moved toward her and peered down. "I can't help who I look like, and I promise you at this point in time,

I don't have one trick up my sleeve. Hell, I didn't even realize I resembled Elvis until I—''

"Resemble? That's an understatement. Am I supposed to believe you're that naive?"

"Lady, I don't care what you believe." He glanced around the room. "It's obvious you and your mother have some kind of hang-up about Elvis Presley. I'd say it goes far beyond being regular fans."

She folded her arms across her chest and jutted out her dimpled chin. The moment she did it, she realized she probably looked exactly like Lou—minus the eye patch. She shook the thought away. "We aren't just fans. We never were *just* fans. We were friends. Or Lou was. And now she wants to keep his memory alive, and she's doing it the best way she knows how." Erin wanted to laugh. Here she was, looking like Lou, sounding like her, defending her.

"Look, you have actions like his. Your voice, the way you say things—that naive, blank look you get now and then. We can tell . . . you've been practicing."

Travor laughed, and turned away from her. "You're as bad as the people sitting out on your front lawn."

"Who coached you?"

"You're like a young pup with a new bone. Tell me, is there a big demand for Elvis impersonators?"

"Don't you know?" she goaded. He didn't answer so she pushed for more information.

"Been out to Vegas lately? Is that where you learned the ropes? They have lots of impersonators out there."

Travor began to pace. She didn't trust him. He didn't know why it mattered, but it was important that he win her trust and the only way he could do that was to tell her the truth. "For your information, I've never been to Vegas. I don't gamble, lie or steal, except in a legal way. I invest in oil wells.''

She laughed. "Oh, I expected that."

He looked surprised. "What do you mean, you expected that?"

"Typical Texan. Doesn't everyone in Texas own an oil well?" I'm being so mean, she thought. Why am I acting this way?

Travor seemed to wilt. His shoulders slumped just a little and she could tell he was racking his brain to come up with something. She bit her tongue. Damn it. Why was she being so mean to him?

"Look, okay, so you're into oil. But why the Elvis persona? What's that all about? I mean . . . you're too good. You got Lou's attention."

"I wasn't trying to."

"You could have fooled me."

"I have," he answered and grinned.

"You have what?"

"Fooled you." He winked. "You think I'm an Elvis impersonator and I'm not."

The wink sent her pulse racing. She felt a flash of heat zoom through her body and inhaled deeply. She didn't want these feelings. She jutted out her chin. "Then I guess you've fooled Lou, too. She might not like that."

"Should I be scared?"

"I wouldn't want to be in your blue suede shoes."

He laughed. "Seriously, what can she do? Force me to wear jumpsuits as long as I'm in Memphis?"

Erin smiled but didn't answer.

"Subject me to meals of nuked bacon and banana sandwiches?"

"Not bad," she murmured.

"Keep me a prisoner in that pink-and-black bedroom of hers?" He shuddered dramatically.

Erin looked at him, cleared her throat, tried to keep the humor out of her voice. "She'll probably book you on 'Larry King Live.'"

"Seriously?" Travor asked, and Erin nodded. He cringed in earnest now. "That's what I was afraid of. Hey, I may look like the guy, but that's as far as it goes."

"Having second thoughts?"

"Believe me, there were never any first thoughts." He sat down beside her. "Your mother makes me nervous. Out of all the Elvis fanatics I've encountered during the past twenty-four hours, for some reason I feel like she's probably the most dangerous. She takes this stuff beyond adoration. I mean, the woman *lives* Elvis."

Erin thought about Lou's scheme to immortalize Elvis Presley. "You're right. Her only goal in the entire world is to keep his memory alive. And she'll go to any length to do it." They looked at each other and Erin smiled her most wicked smile. "Mr. Steele, you probably won't leave this house alive."

Travor smiled back and eased his arm around the back of the sofa. "Then I'll have to insist, Ms. Weller, that you grant me one last wish." He pulled her toward him and kissed her.

She was lost. Her head spun as his arms enveloped her. She wanted to push him away—in fact, she thought she had—but at the same time, she seemed to be pulling him closer. His ravenous mouth captured hers; or was it the other way around? Lord, she hadn't kissed anyone in so long. She hadn't wanted anyone in so long. She hadn't loved anyone since . . .

Fire coursed through her veins. She heard her pounding heart and wondered at the intensity of it. Never had her heart beat so out of control. So loudly. Could Travor hear it, too? He must—

Then she opened her eyes and looked into the face of a little man in uniform. She pushed Travor away and screamed, fearing as much for him as for herself. A crazed fan could be very dangerous.

"Travor—" she began, but he'd jumped up and had grabbed the little man by the collar.

"Okay, buddy, what do you want? How'd you get in here?"

The odd-looking stranger sputtered and croaked. Unable to speak, he poked a plastic Elvis toward them. Erin gasped as she recognized Lou's outrageous keychain invention, and the house key dangling from Elvis's head.

"Oh, no. What has she done now?" she groaned, jumping up from the sofa. "Let him go, Travor. Lou sent him."

The little man coughed and sputtered as he straightened his jacket. When he was finished, he looked at Erin. "I knocked. Honest, I knocked on the door for a long time."

So much for my loud, pounding heart, she thought. She could feel the heat penetrate her face but she didn't dare look at Travor. "So why are you here?" she asked.

"I been hired to deliver a limo to—" He paused and stared hard at Travor. Then he swallowed twice before adding, "The King."

Chapter Five

"I understand your mother wanting to keep his memory alive, Erin, but couldn't she just wear a T-shirt with his picture on it?"

Erin giggled nervously as they hurried through the crowd of people on their front lawn. Travor was a tall man, but he almost seemed dwarfed beside the four men Lou had sent to "guard" him. Erin had to run to match their long strides.

When they reached the white limousine, the men surrounded both Erin and Travor as they entered. The long car squealed away from the Weller house, and Erin turned to see several of the fans running toward their own cars while others sat down in the grass to wait. She sighed. It was going to be a long day.

"Are you with Phillips Security?" she asked the huge bodyguard nearest them.

"Yeah, we're here for as long as we're needed."

"Hopefully that won't be too long," Erin mumbled. She knew exactly how much Lou had already spent hiring the four bodyguards and the limousine. A small fortune. A fortune they didn't have. And Lou knew better. Why was she doing this? They didn't need a limo. They didn't need bodyguards.

"Would you mind telling me what the hell is going on now?" Travor asked.

Erin shook her head. "I think we have Lou's version of the Memphis Mafia. They're supposed to keep you out of harm's way, stand between you and the so-called gate people."

Travor squirmed uneasily. "This whole thing gives me the willies." He bent close to Erin and whispered. "Look at the way these guys are watching me."

"Get used to it," she whispered back.

Travor sat up and frowned at her. "Okay, what the hell are gate people? Ya'll don't even have a gate."

"Very astute, Mr. Steele," she answered sarcastically, but Travor darkened his already dark glare. Erin realized he was just as put out as she was. "Back in the so-called good old days, gate people were Elvis fans who had a ritual of standing outside his gate. They seemed to have their own little club and they were known for taking things a step further than the normal Elvis fan."

"Meaning what? That they got violent?"

"Lou swears they were never violent."

"Then why are bodyguards necessary? I don't want them. I don't need them."

"Believe me, as long as you're in town, they're necessary." Listen to me, she thought. I'm falling right in there with Lou's way of thinking. "Have you already forgotten what happened at that burger joint? And Lou wasn't even around then."

Travor grunted. "That's hard to believe. I wouldn't be a bit surprised to find she'd rigged that, too. Where are we going, anyway?"

Erin leaned forward and looked around. "I'll bet you ten to one we're on our way to the studio, so just sit back and relax."

"Relax? You've got to be kidding." Travor folded his arms across his chest and looked out the window. Did these women actually believe he was going to let them railroad him into becoming Elvis Presley the Second? No way. He took a deep breath and cleared his throat. In a deep, firm voice, he said, "I hesitate to bring this up... it's such a minor detail...."

He watched as Erin turned to look at him, her eyes so clear and blue, he almost lost his train of thought.

"But no one has *asked* me if I'm *willing* to participate in this project."

He turned back toward the window, savoring the surprised look on her face.

The studio wasn't exactly what he had expected. Oh, it was pink and black, all right, but tastefully so. And it was decorated with more than just Elvis memorabilia. There were certificates and awards lining one wall, while pictures of Carl Perkins, Jerry Lee Lewis, and several people Travor didn't recognize lined another. Travor wanted desperately to check out the certificates; see if these women had any credentials at all. He couldn't help but doubt it.

"So you finally got here!" Lou greeted them. She was perched on the end of the secretary's credenza but she popped up and hustled toward them. "We got your clothes, Travor. There's a fee for getting your bike back. Sorry, I didn't have the cash."

Travor took the duffel bag Max was holding. "That's okay, Ms. Weller. I can—"

"Call me Lou." She took his arm and moved him toward a couple of ladies he assumed were employees.

Travor reluctantly let her guide him, very aware that Erin had disappeared inside an office without speaking to anyone. "Okay, Lou. I'm glad to know my bike is safe. When we leave here, you can drop me wherever it is and I'll—"

Lou interrupted again. "Did you meet your boys? They look pretty tough, don't they? Let me introduce you around. Travor Steele, this is..."

Erin came out of an office, tying a denim wraparound skirt at her waist. She kept extra clothes—dressy and casual—because she never knew when she might need to change her attire to fit a specific occasion. She picked up a stack of mail and shuffled through it, keeping one ear attuned to Lou's chatter. Bills, bills and more bills. She wondered how Lou had been able to lease or rent the limo, and how she'd talked Lyon Phillips out of four bodyguards. Lord, Lou and her silver tongue. But Lou was tangled up in a failure chain and something was going to have to break. And it'll have to be more than just another Elvis look-alike, Erin thought. They'd been doing fairly well until a couple of years ago when Lou sank everything they had into a movie-of-the-week venture about an Elvis fanatic. That was the beginning of their demise. One thing led to another and now they were so far in debt, they couldn't pay attention, as the joke went. But the joke was true, and not very funny. Erin was so preoccupied with their finances, trying to keep them afloat, save their home and business while raising her kid single-handedly, that she really did have a difficult time paying attention. And that affected her work, her concentration. They needed a miracle, and she didn't think Travor Steele was that miracle.

She heard her mother introducing Travor to everyone, including the so-called Memphis Mafia. She could hear Max encouraging him to give them a name. "How about the Texas Quatros?" Max asked. Erin wrinkled her nose and stifled a giggle.

Come on, kiddo, get creative. You can do better than that, she mentally encouraged. She loved listening to Max and Lou brainstorm ideas and moneymaking schemes. She liked the way they tried to outdo each other, the way they challenged each other to think. Unfortunately, this time, even if they came up with a viable, foolproof scheme, she'd have to veto it. They couldn't finance it; they absolutely could not sink one more penny into Travor Steele or Elvis Presley. The end of Star Music Studio was a real fear this time; it could actually happen.

In spite of their clients, and their many successes, they'd had far too many bad investments and failures. How could one handsome Elvis look-alike make a difference now? He couldn't. It was too late.

Erin leaned against the desk, watching as Travor talked to the employees standing around him. He looked comfortable in the black leather—just like Elvis speaking with his fans. As if he felt her eyes on him, he turned and stared at her. Her body grew warm under his gaze. Suddenly, he put his hand up and she heard him say he'd like to change, get into something a little more respectable. Everyone laughed and Max escorted Travor down the hall.

"Can't you just see him in a music video?" Lou asked, coming up beside Erin and leaning against the wall.

Erin didn't look at her mother. She was so angry she could hardly speak. "We can't afford it, Lou. Just like we can't afford the bodyguards or the limo. Why did you do it?"

"For the publicity. The more attention he gets, the better for us. We can't afford not to do this," Lou answered and raised her glittery eye patch. "Videos are hot right now. What if we do something like Hank Williams, Jr., did? Remember that video where he's supposedly singing with his father? We could have Travor singing with Elvis. Two Elvises. We could—"

"Please! No more!" Erin put her hands over her ears in mock horror as much to harass Lou as to keep the word *videos* from reverberating throughout her head. Videos... If they only had the money. But they didn't and that was a fact. "Lou, we don't know a thing about videos. That would mean hiring directors, choreographers, photographers—the works. Besides, you don't have your star yet."

Lou laughed. "I will have him. And whatever we do, I'm going all the way this time. I want it to be a real tribute to Elvis, and ensure his place in the years to come. I don't want him to ever be forgotten."

"Oh, Lou, you know he'll never be forgotten. He's a legend."

An obstinate look crossed Lou's face. She let the fake eye-patch slap against her eye. "Sure, every time someone sings one of his songs, he's remembered. Every time someone pops a joke about him, he's remembered. That's not good enough. I hate those jokes. The man deserves respect... from everyone."

Erin realized that further talk against Lou's project would be like spitting in the wind. She tried another tactic. "Okay, think about this. You've got a country boy from Rattan, Texas. Granted, he looks absolutely great but how can you possibly pull off anything grand? To be successful it'll have to be big, it'll have to be entirely new . . . never done before. It will cost a fortune. We don't have a fortune. We don't have anything." She held up her hand when Lou tried to protest. *"Except* a good-looking Elvis look-alike who'd be a dream in videos."

Lou surprised Erin by sighing deeply, looking for all the world like a deflated balloon. "I'm gonna need your help, Erin. I don't have one good idea."

Erin wanted to laugh, then she wanted to cry. It was this vulnerable side of Lou that always got to her. "Oh, Lou, this whole thing is ludicrous."

"You can believe what you want to believe, call me crazy and pooh-pooh the whole scheme but I can spot a star. In all the others something was missing. That special ingredient. This country boy from Rattan has it."

"Has what?" came a voice from the hall. Both Erin and Lou whirled to stare at him. He wore faded jeans and a red Western shirt.

Lou quickly took Travor's arm and moved him toward the rear of the studio. "Come on and I'll tell you all about it."

Erin watched them walk away from her. Caught up in the broadness of his shoulders, the narrowness of his hips, she had to admit, Lou was right. He would look damned good in videos.

She could visualize a stark-white background with a blurred image belting out a no-fail hit in Elvis's versa-

tile, powerful voice. The sexy image would only come
into focus at the end of the song, a startling revelation
to see Elvis in the nineties. The idea had punch but
they'd need a song that couldn't fail, maybe something
by George Jones; his were nearly always hits. She felt
her skin tingle. Of course, it would have to be handled
properly. But could they pull it off with an unknown?
And would Travor be willing?

An angry loud voice yanked Erin out of her reverie.
"So this is why you didn't have time to meet with me?
You're grooming new talent, aren't you? Does he know
you're going belly-up?"

Erin shot a quick look toward Travor and Lou and
shook her head in warning. Just what she needed—a
Kimbie Love temper tantrum. Erin didn't want Lou and
this temperamental young singer tangling yet again.
And she certainly didn't want Travor interceding on
anyone's behalf as he seemed prone to do at times.

"Now, Kimbie—"

"Cut the crap, Ms. Weller. There're just too many
tales floating around—there's got to be some truth to
them. You're busted, aren't you? That's why you
haven't done anything for me."

"We haven't—" Erin began, but the flashy red-
haired singer interrupted her again.

"You're absolutely right. You haven't, and now it's
too late. I'm not going to waste any more time with your
broken-down little studio. I thought because you were
small I'd get more attention. Well, I haven't gotten *any*
attention."

"Kimbie—"

"Don't *Kimbie* me. This is exactly what I think of
you, your mother and Star Music Studio." In a threat-

ening manner, she held up what was obviously her contract.

Erin grabbed the young woman's arm. "Get a grip, Kimbie, you're about to blow a very important deal." She turned her head toward Travor Steele and gave a slight nod. The young singer followed Erin's gaze and squinted.

"You mean he's here to—"

"Don't say another word, Kimbie. Things are at a very precarious stage. We aren't certain we can work it out...but if we can...it'll be big...for all of us. That's a guarantee."

Kimbie Love gave Travor another look. "He sure is a hunk, but haven't I seen him somewhere before?"

Erin stifled a grin. "He just flew in from the West Coast. Under the circumstances, I don't think I should introduce you now—"

Kimbie blushed and apologized profusely. "Oh, God, I hope I didn't screw anything up. Me and my big mouth. I'm so sorry, Erin. I just— You know how impatient I get. Sometimes I just don't think."

Erin turned Kimbie toward the door. "I know. You need to work on that. Patience is everything in this business. So is timing."

"Oh, I hope I didn't blow it."

"I hope not too, Kimbie, but let's learn something from this. Your temper, your violent outbursts could be very detrimental to your career." She nodded again toward Travor and Lou. "I promise you, you're going places. We'll see to that."

When Kimbie left, Erin closed her eyes and wondered what in the world she was going to do to promote Kimbie Love. The woman had a very sensual voice, it gave Erin chills to hear her sing, but there was something wrong in her presentation as well as her personality.

"Like mother, like daughter," Lou teased in a singsong voice, as she moved toward Erin.

Erin pushed away from the door, giving a mock bow. "Thanks for the compliment, Lou, but compliments don't pay the rent. You should be working on something for her instead of playing around with Elvis.

"She's your discovery, not mine."

"I know. You keep reminding me. Well, here's something for you to think about, *partner.* If we don't come up with something super fantastic for our spoiled Ms. Love, we're *both* going to be giving tours at Sun Studio."

Lou gave a mock shiver. Then she grinned. "We have a gold mine at our fingertips." They turned and looked at Travor who was leaning against the wall, looking extremely handsome with his hands shoved in his pockets.

"Travor?" Erin asked. She wasn't really asking anything or expecting an answer. She just wanted to feel the name on her lips, as if by saying it, she was giving credence to her mother's opinion.

He shrugged and shook his head. "Don't look at me, sweet thing. I haven't got a clue."

The ride back to the Weller house was quiet, rather solemn. Erin frowned out the window, deep in thought. Travor wondered if she was replaying the scene with that Kimbie Love person. He had—several times. He hadn't realized Erin could be as sly as her mother. He wondered if Erin even realized it. She'd smoothly taken control of a bad situation and turned it around, bought Star Music Studio more time. And from the sound of things, that was exactly what they needed: more time and certainly more money. Travor mulled over everything he'd seen and heard. So they were busted. Broke. In dire need of money to save their sinking ship. In spite of his glib comment back at the studio, he did indeed have a clue. They needed him. But as much as he liked Erin and her son—even her wacky mother—he wasn't sure he wanted to get involved. Maybe he could make them a loan, then be on his way. He had a feeling he was going to get in way over his head.

With the dinner dishes piled in the sink, Travor, Lou, Erin and Max had retired to the living area to "take care of business," as Lou put it.

Travor rubbed his chin. "Tell me, just what is it you want me to do? Let's get to the point of this conversation."

Lou took a deep breath. "I want to make a series of videos that can compete with anything being aired today."

"Hey, cool idea, Grandma!" Max yelled, then ran across the room, toward the kitchen.

Lou grinned when she heard him slam through the back door. "He's right. It is a cool idea."

Travor shook his head, and Lou continued.

"You don't need to panic, Travor. There's nothing worse than a bad Elvis impersonator, but you got it, kiddo. You got what it takes."

"Except experience," Erin said.

"Except experience," Lou conceded. "But you don't need experience because if you have that, then you've lost the innocence, the freshness that I want to capture."

Erin shook her head. "A series, Lou? You said you didn't have any new ideas."

Lou shrugged. "I don't. I'm just tossing things around. I haven't really figured anything out yet."

"You haven't figured it out? No new ideas? You're aiming for the big time with no ideas?" Travor got up from his chair and ran a hand through his hair. He began to pace. "Is this another Kimbie Love deal?"

Erin and Lou looked at each other.

"Yeah, I heard what the redhead said. To use her words, you've gone belly-up."

"Not yet," Lou answered.

"But not far from it," Travor challenged.

Lou sat forward on the edge of her seat. "Look, videos always do well."

Travor held up a hand. "Okay, maybe so, but let's get back to the 'no ideas' part. From what I understand, Kimbie Love isn't real satisfied—"

"I didn't want to sign her on. She's Erin's baby."

Erin had been waiting for that. "And she's a darn good performer. The problem is...sometimes she's rather offensive."

"Yeah," Lou agreed. "She tends to throw temper tantrums at the oddest times. Like right before a benefit performance at Baptist Memorial Hospital."

Erin sighed, then looked at Travor. "I was listening to demo tapes and Kimbie's was one of them. She really has a fantastic voice but she's blowing it. Her personality is destroying her career."

Travor walked away from them, then turned and studied them both. "Look, there's something I'm having trouble with. Aren't you two partners?"

"Sure we are. We discuss everything," Lou answered.

"But we don't always agree," Erin explained.

"Maybe this is why Star Music Studio is going under—because you two aren't working together."

"We do work together," Lou argued. "We just have different approaches. Erin usually has things all worked out in her head or on paper before she makes a deal. I tend to make the deal, then work things out in my head. I'm the risk taker," she explained proudly.

Travor looked at Erin for confirmation; she shrugged. He shook his head and spoke directly to Lou. "I'm not used to doing business this way."

"It'll work," Lou insisted. "It's worked before."

Erin got up from her chair. "But not this time. Because we can't afford any unnecessary risks." She looked at Lou. "We have to be certain, we have to plan, Lou, or we'll lose everything."

"That won't happen. We won't let it. We can—"

"Tell me this," Travor interrupted. "How do you know Elvis could have made it in today's world? From the sound on my radio, music's changed a lot."

Lou was quick to answer. "Elvis is still the King. He was the best. People still buy his music. He could've made it in today's world, and I can prove that with you."

"The idea of making a fool of myself is very unappealing."

Lou shot Erin a "Help me" look, then turned back to Travor. "You just leave things to us. You can do it. I saw you do it. We all saw you. You mimicked his expressions. Your voice is almost exactly like his. You're sexy. He's sexy, isn't he, Erin?"

Travor blushed; so did Erin.

Lou waved her hand toward the bookcase. "I have everything you need. There are documentaries, all his movies, every book written about him. You can study those before we even get started. Erin can train you. By the time she's finished with you, you won't know if you're Travor Steele or Elvis Presley."

"Lou, I can't!" She couldn't train Travor Steele to be an Elvis impersonator. Just being near him made her feel young and giddy. Her heart pumped in her ears. Her skin tingled. And she broke out in hot flashes that had nothing to do with age or menopause. How did Lou expect her to conduct business when she could barely look at the guy? Thank God, he had some sense. She knew he wouldn't buy it.

"How long do you think it would take for Erin to train me?" Travor asked.

Erin felt a chill slide up her spine. Oh, God, would he actually consider it?

"Sugar, if you can mimic the man with no training at all, then I'd say you're halfway there," Lou replied.

Travor moved closer to Lou and sat down on the edge of the sofa. "Look, Ms. Weller—Lou. For the record, I didn't come here to be discovered. And I really have some reservations about this." He looked at Erin and his gaze lingered for a moment. He turned back to Lou. "Then again, I have to admit something about this project appeals to me."

Erin gulped and they both looked at her. No one said a word.

Travor continued. "But the very thought of being before a camera makes me feel like a fool."

Lou waved a hand at him, as if to brush off his insecurities. She was about to speak when Max burst into the room.

"There's a man outside wants to know when you're gonna plug the phones back in."

Lou jumped up from her chair. "I wondered why those phones weren't ringing. Smart move, Erin. Buying us some time." She turned to Max. "Tell him in one hour." She grinned. "We can always use time. Time and money are two very precious commodities. Now, Travor Steele, what I want you to do is—"

"Please, let me say something first. I've got to be back in Texas within the next day or two."

Lou grinned from ear to ear and raised her eye patch high up on her forehead. "Perfect. That's no problem at all. Just take Erin with you and she can teach you everything you need to know."

Erin jumped up from her chair. "Ohh, no, you don't," she said, moving toward her mother. "I've got other things to do. I've got to get Max into that tutoring program for math, finish up the jingles for Jan's Bakery and I'm still negotiating with Bud on the supermarket promotion and—"

"I'll take care of Max and you can play with your jingles in Texas. How about it, Max? Can't we make it a few days without her?"

"Sure, Grandma. We can handle anything."

"Even Kimbie Love?" Erin challenged.

Max and Lou looked at each other and made a face.

Erin shook her head and met her mother's eyes. "Don't do this, Lou. I know what's going on inside your head. It won't work."

Lou grinned broadly, and let the bright piece of leather slap against her eye. She wrapped an arm around Max and whispered something. Max laughed. Then they raised their arms and pretended to be pounding drums.

Da-dum, da-dum, da-dum, dum, dum.

As loudly as they could, they marched around the room singing, "The eyes of Texas are upon you, all the—" then disappeared into the kitchen.

Chapter Six

"I don't like you playing Cupid, Lou. I can handle my own relationships."

"What relationships? You've never had a relationship. You've only had a rebellious period and a bad experience."

The two of them were continuing their argument from the night before.

"I don't want to talk about it anymore. Are you sure you packed the *Viva Las Vegas* tape? It wasn't with the others, you know. And I want to take Kimbie Love's demo."

Lou put a hand on her daughter's shoulder. "Erin, calm down. Everything you need is packed. And you're going to do fine."

Erin slumped against the wall. "I'm not worried about the training. I'm worried about—" She didn't finish. How could she tell Lou that she was worried about being alone with Travor? That every time he looked at her, her blood boiled in her veins. That every time he smiled, her heart pumped violently. A girl didn't tell her mother those kinds of things—even a mother like Lou.

"You like him, don't you?"

Erin jerked her eyes toward Lou and wondered if she'd been thinking aloud. "No... not the way you think."

"You like him," Lou repeated. "Exactly the way I think—you just don't want to admit it. It's time for you to put Kyle Duncan out of your mind, Erin. I would say 'heart' but he was never in your heart. It's time you realize that."

"I loved Kyle. And he loved me."

Lou shook her head. "It was just teenage—"

"Grandma, look!"

Erin and Lou exchanged a look, silently agreeing to drop the subject. Max entered the room, followed by Travor who was dressed in faded jeans, a Don't Mess With Texas T-shirt and running shoes. Both Lou and Erin started at his feet and worked their way up. They gasped when they got to his face. His sideburns had disappeared and before them stood a young man who could very well have played the lead role in *King Creole* or *Love Me Tender*.

"I told him not to do it," Max said.

Erin burst into uncontrollable laughter.

"Hey, do I look that funny?" Travor asked, grinning a silly, lopsided grin that would have appeared quite dumb on anyone else. "I thought this might make things a little easier for us to get out of town. I'm not taking those bodyguards."

Trying to temper her giggles, Erin turned to look at Lou, who was white as a sheet and shaking her head.

"You almost screwed up," Lou said. "Instead of bold and flashy we'll have to go young and naive—kinda like Clint, huh, Erin?"

"They could be twins." Erin looked at Travor mischievously, then immediately looked away. "He's amazing, Lou. Travor can be any Elvis character you want him to be."

"What are ya'll talking about? Who's Clint?" Travor asked.

Lou answered. "Clint was the character Elvis played in *Love Me Tender.* How old did you say you are?" she asked.

"I'll be thirty-one in a couple of months. Why?"

Lou moved away from him, not answering. "You need to watch some Elvis movies. What you've succeeded in doing is becoming a younger, more vulnerable, Presley look-alike. As far as making it easier to get out of town, I don't know that you're any better off than you were." She shook her head again. "That's not exactly the look I wanted, but we're lucky. Hair'll grow back." She looked at Erin. "Let's have some breakfast so you two can get on the road. Just promise me one thing: don't let him go blond, Erin. I never did like that yellow-haired Elvis in *Kissin' Cousins.*

Two hours later, Erin was driving south on Interstate 55. I've got to be out of my mind, she thought, and pressed her foot to the gas pedal. The guy turns my blood to boiling goop, and here I am leaving town with him, crossing three states. A quiver of uncertainty hovered in the pit of her stomach. How am I going to be able to resist him?

"What are you thinking about?"

Erin glanced over at Travor, sitting in the passenger seat. In spite of the distance between them, she felt his body heat; or was it her imagination? She frowned, pushing the thought away. "I was thinking that if I had a normal mother, none of this would be happening."

Travor laughed. "I'm sure you're right. But just think what an exciting life you've had."

"Yeah, exciting. If there's one thing we know for sure, it's that we *don't* know what's going to happen from day to day."

"Sure beats a routine existence." Travor sighed.

"Want to trade?"

He threw back his head, laughing in a way Erin hadn't seen him do. At this moment, he looked about as much like Elvis Presley as she did. Was it possible they were making a mistake? Could Lou's instincts be wrong?

"You know, I really shouldn't be leaving Memphis."

"Why?"

"It makes me nervous to let Lou out of my sight. You saw how long it took her to cut a deal with bodyguards and the limo. Do you think she's going to sit quietly while we're out of town?" She rolled her eyes and shook her head. "I don't think so."

Travor straightened in the bucket seat. "What could she do?"

Erin glanced at him again. "Are you kidding? She can do anything she wants to do. You should know that by now."

Erin had pulled Max aside and warned him to let her know if Lou started cooking up some media hype. And she'd specifically warned Lou to stay away from the banks and the loan sharks, and not to sell the house while she was away. But who knew what her mother would do? Lou always had things her way. Always.

Travor shifted again. "I don't want to think about it. Let's change the subject. You ever been to New Orleans?"

"I've been to the Superdome several times for concerts, but I've never been down in the French Quarter. Does that count?"

"The life you've lived and you've never been in the French Quarter?"

"I've never been *anywhere* strictly as a tourist."

"Then we'll spend the night there. For one whole day and a night, you'll be a tourist. My treat."

Erin felt that hot little quiver start in the pit of her stomach and zoom its way up to her breasts. It was becoming a familiar feeling to her. "No, I don't think so—"

"That was my original plan, anyway—to see New Orleans."

"But what about the business you have to take care of?"

"Another day or two won't matter that much."

She shot him a suspicious look. "I got the impression you were anxious to get home. Isn't that what you led Lou to believe?"

"Well, I was but I'm not too far off schedule. We can do a little sight-seeing. How about it?"

Erin didn't dare look at him. His sultry voice, his gentle ways, that lopsided grin and those sweet-looking lips had tempted her to leave town with him in the first place, venture into the unknown.

Even now, while speeding down Interstate 55, she felt a tingling in her limbs. Her nerves sizzled as if they were about to explode. Any moment something was going to happen to her; she could feel it. A vision popped into her head: one hotel room, one king-size bed, one man and one woman wrapped in each other's arms.

A bubble of anticipation floated up from her stomach, exploded and shot through her like a Roman candle. Just as quickly, another vision replaced it: the memory of a seventeen-year-old girl in the maternity ward of St. Joseph Hospital in Albuquerque, New Mexico. She eased her foot from the gas pedal as a film of apprehension settled over her.

Travor looked down at her sneakered foot, frowned, then gazed out the window of the van. They'd just driven through Jackson and she'd been pushing the odometer over the speed limit until he'd mentioned spending the night in New Orleans. He wondered why. Because she didn't want to waste the time, or because of him? He glanced down at her foot again. Her jeans were rolled up and knotted in some weird manner, displaying just a peek of her ankle. The paleness of her skin sent a pleasant sensation through him. She'd run around most of yesterday in shorts and he'd recorded every detail: a mole on her thigh, a scar just below her knee, a razor nick on her shin. Her graceful curves and sleek lines had tempted, tormented him unmercifully— and they still did.

He shifted and stared out the window again. Frowning, he made a mental note to be damned careful. He couldn't make a mistake like he had with Celeste. That had been a real catastrophe. One he'd never forget. He twisted the diamond ring on his little finger. Good times with no strings. That was all he wanted. He looked down at that pale slim ankle again and his blood heated. Damn, why had he agreed to bring her home with him?

He'd felt certain if he told Lou he had to return to East Texas, she'd cancel everything. But when she'd suggested Erin accompany him—how could he refuse? They'd be together and they'd be alone. Still . . . The thought of portraying Elvis Presley made him feel foolish. Would he be able to do it? Could he? Should he? He pushed the thought from his mind. He didn't want to worry about Lou or Elvis or what the future might bring. Not yet, anyway.

Looking Erin up and down as she drove the van, Travor grinned. "You know, things could be a lot worse."

"How's that?" she asked.

"I could be stuck on this boring highway with one of those muscle-bound bodyguards."

She shot him a smile. "Thanks . . . I think."

"You're welcome."

Erin kept her eyes on the road but Travor seemed excessively interested in the scenery, dull as it was. He pointed out abandoned houses, wondering aloud why a family would move away, leave a home that seemed, at least from the outside, structurally sound. He commented on everything he saw—fields of cattle, construction sites, littered ditches and dead animals. At one point, Erin had adamantly vetoed picking up a hitchhiker.

"According to the sign he was waving, the guy was just going to the next town. Why couldn't we give him a ride?"

"I picked you up and look what happened. I've learned my lesson."

Another time, she'd just as adamantly refused to rescue a stray dog with three puppies.

"You're really a hard-hearted woman, Erin. Anyone who'd pass by starving pups . . ."

"There's no way I'm going to let four dogs loose in this van. I can just imagine the smell. And they'd chew the upholstery."

She'd wanted to tell Travor she thought he had enough animals from the sounds that came across the telephone when she'd talked to Nellie, but she didn't want him to know she'd called, checked up on him. On top of being a bleeding heart for every stray on the side of the highway, Travor wanted to read every historical marker they passed, and he insisted on stopping every hour to get out of the van and stretch his legs. He was an unusual traveling companion, so unlike Lou who packed the portable potty, snacks galore, and refused to stop for anything other than gas. This guy is going to drive Lou wild, Erin thought, and stifled a giggle.

They finally connected with Interstate 10 that would take them into New Orleans. Travor was driving and it was early afternoon. Erin was holding a map and several brochures she'd taken from a tourist bureau at the state line.

"We should be there in about half an hour," Travor informed her. "What do you want to do first, sightsee or find a place to stay?"

"Sightsee," she answered too quickly. Travor looked at her and grinned. She grinned back, mockingly. She wondered if he knew, if he understood that the very thought of checking into a hotel with him sent panic waves gushing through her. The vision of the single room, the king-size bed was growing clearer in her mind. Did he have the same vision?

She cleared her mind and stared out the window at the swampy scenery. Cypress knees jutted from the murky water, and turtles sunned themselves on logs.

White long-legged birds perched about, looking like yard decorations.

Too soon they reached New Orleans.

Traffic was heavy despite the hour, and Travor drove cautiously. Before they realized it, they saw a sign that read St. Charles Avenue.

"Look! That's our exit!" Erin yelled.

Travor whipped to the right, almost clipping a shiny stretch limousine. "Sorry about that," he said, rubbing a hand on his jeans. He laughed. "Do you think it was Elvis?"

"No, it looked like Lou!"

"What?" He jerked around.

Although her tone of voice had been serious, a smile played around her lips. "I told you not to put anything past her."

He grinned. "Cute. That was real cute."

They made their way through narrow streets and soon ended up in downtown New Orleans. After fumbling around like lost tourists, Travor pulled into a pay parking-lot. "I give up trying to drive in this traffic. Let's walk. We'll find a place to stay later."

Erin nodded, saying a silent prayer to the powers that be. She wasn't ready to deal with the issue of one room or two.

They locked the van and stood on the sidewalk for a moment, surveying their whereabouts. Travor grabbed her hand.

"Let's follow those people up ahead. They're wearing New York T-shirts so they're bound to be tourists. They'll lead us into the French Quarter—I hope."

The sidewalks were rough with uneven bricks. Pedestrians pushed by them as if they had some place important to go. Travor pointed out that tourists rubbernecked in awe while the natives kept their eyes focused straight ahead.

"How do you know so much about it?" Erin challenged.

Travor faked an offended look. "You don't think I'd take off on my motorcycle without doing some research, do you? Just ask me something, anything, and I'll bet I can answer it."

Erin waved him away, laughing.

But soon they came into a more congested area and Erin eased closer to Travor. She didn't like being surrounded by so many people. It reminded her of concert crowds, Lou pulling and pushing her between bodies so thick she could smell their sweat. Travor put his arm around her shoulders, guided her gently. She felt a little safer.

"This must be the famous Jackson Square." He seemed as excited as a schoolboy and leaned close to her ear. She felt his breath hot against the side of her face and it sent her pulse racing. "Let's walk around awhile. We have plenty of time before we find a place to stay." With his hands on her shoulders, he pushed her forward, ahead of him.

The square was filled with artists, street people, musicians and tourists. There seemed to Erin to be an unusual mixture of everything. Some of the entertainers were mere children, tap-dancing to music blaring from a radio. Others were old men, sitting on buckets while plucking guitars. Every performer had a hat or a coffee can before him with money sticking from it.

The architecture fluctuated from Spanish to French and was decorated with wrought or cast iron. Above, balconies dripped with colorful plastic beads or greenery, and on several, couples stood, sipping cool drinks and eyeing the tourists below.

"Let's get something to drink," Erin said, fanning herself. She pointed to an outdoor café.

"Café du Monde. A very famous place," he said, imitating a Cajun accent. They crossed Decatur Street, walked beneath the arch with its green-and-white awnings and into the open café. They selected a round table situated beneath a ceiling fan. The little bit of breeze felt good on Erin's face and neck.

A pretty young waitress appeared immediately, seeking their orders.

"Beignets," Travor answered the woman. "Two orders and coffee." He turned to Erin. "It's a tourist rule, beignets and café au lait in New Orleans."

Erin smiled. "But I want something cold. No coffee for me." She ordered a cola and wiped at her brow with the back of her hand, noting that Travor seemed completely comfortable with the humidity. Although his hair was slightly mussed, there was certainly no perspiration on his brow. He looked every bit the cool, collected Elvis impersonator.

The waitress returned carrying one saucer with six very large, heavily powdered confections piled high.

Travor looked a little embarrassed. "That's an awful lot. We just had two orders," he told the waitress.

"This is two orders," she repeated and pointed.

"It looks more like four," Travor mumbled.

Erin grinned. The waitress disappeared.

"Two orders," Travor mimicked and held up four fingers. He squinted his eyes, stretched his neck, and grinned real big. "You're a redneck if you can't tell the difference between one order and two."

Erin gasped. "Hey, how did you do that? You sound just like Jeff Foxworthy."

He repeated his performance.

"You're a—" She paused as if recalling everything he'd said and done in the past forty-eight hours, then she squinted her eyes. "You *are* an impersonator. That's why you could so easily slip into the Elvis persona." Her suspicions returned.

"Now get that look off your face," Travor admonished. "I'm *not* a professional entertainer, and I'm *not* trying to get discovered. It's just something I've always been able to do."

Erin wasn't convinced. "No one can 'just do' impersonations. It takes a lot of hard work." Yet, she knew he was telling the truth. The guy knew very little about Elvis. "Okay, explain it to me."

He tweaked her nose. "I will—someday."

"You said you sing—"

"No. *You* said I sing. I told you I had a tape and you assumed it was my singing."

She sat up straighter. "Then what was on that tape if it wasn't your singing?"

Travor bit into the crisp fritter and powdered sugar went everywhere. Erin laughed. Before she realized what she was doing, she reached out and brushed the white powder from the side of his cheek.

Their eyes met and Erin felt the sparks between them. Her heart pounded as she pulled her hand away. Damn, she shouldn't have touched him. Things were bad enough without that.

"Come on, what was on the tape?" she whispered, trying to get control of her body.

Travor smiled, as if he understood exactly what she was doing. "I made it for a friend. He's in a wheelchair, doesn't do any traveling, so it's tales of what I've seen on this trip. I did it in celebrity voices.''

"Oh," Erin mumbled. She felt foolish. She'd over-reacted, assumed Travor was trying to be discovered because of his Presley looks. Instead, he'd been helping a disabled friend who couldn't travel. She looked down at the table. "You must think I'm an idiot."

He reached over and took her chin between his thumb and forefinger. "I would never think you're an idiot. I could have explained at any time, but you were so caught up in your suspicions, I wanted to see how far you'd take it." He brushed her bottom lip with his thumb.

She pulled away, tried not to notice the heat emanating from where he'd touched her. "I took it pretty far, didn't I?"

Travor grinned. "Yeah, but it was fun."

She turned away from him, looked toward the concrete steps that would take them up on the levee. A young man was aiming a camera at them; he clicked off several frames. Erin felt the back of her neck tingle, but she brushed the warning away. She turned back to Travor, and watched him drink his coffee, tap the powdered sugar off his beignet before he bit into it. *I'm glad he isn't seeking stardom. I'm glad he's a nobody.* But for some reason, she felt they were back to square one, and she couldn't help but wonder why.

They'd walked up and down the streets of the Vieux Carré. Travor had left his camera in his duffel bag back in the van so he purchased a disposable one and had snapped picture after picture: Erin, posed in front of the Andrew Jackson statue. Erin, nose-to-nose with a behatted donkey. Erin, trying to make a white-faced mime crack a smile.

Every now and then, they were approached by other tourists who wanted their picture taken with the Elvis impersonator. Travor seemed happy to oblige, and Erin couldn't help but notice how he enjoyed the attention. He'd throw an arm around the women and look like best buddies with the men. He had the makings of a great entertainer.

"You know, Elvis was in New Orleans. They filmed *King Creole* here."

"I've never seen it." They were walking through the garden park in front of the St. Louis Cathedral.

"Have you seen *any* of his movies?" she asked.

"I think I saw the one of him in the army."

"*King Creole* was one of his best. The story line was taken from a Harold Robbins novel and the part Elvis played was originally meant for James Dean."

For the first time, Travor acted impressed. "But James Dean seems like a whole different personality."

"He was—but then again, maybe he wasn't. I don't think Elvis ever really had a fair chance with his movies. Books about his life say he was offered the costarring role in *A Star Is Born*. Can you picture him playing opposite Barbra Streisand? And they say he was wanted for a remake of *Thunder Road*. Can you just imagine Elvis playing a bootlegger? But what if he had? Just think of it—his entire life would have been different."

Travor looked at her closely. "Listen to yourself. You're getting excited...just by thinking of the what if or what could have been. Do you realize you sound just like Lou?"

"I guess Lou and I share some traits," she said somewhat defensively.

They took a carriage ride, a street-car tour and hit every little souvenir shop within the square. Travor insisted on buying several dozen alligator claws to mail back to Max.

"Six dozen for five dollars. I don't know what an alligator claw is worth but Max is an enterprising little man. He'll probably get three bucks apiece for them," he mused. "One more purchase," he said, and steered Erin down the block to Aunt Sally's Pralines.

"What do you think?" he asked. "Two dozen, three? Lou won't OD on them, will she?"

"Her taste buds will go wild," Erin said. They gave the shopkeeper Lou's address, then drifted into the heart of the French Quarter where Travor stopped to watch a couple strumming a guitar and singing. When they finished their song, Travor stuffed a twenty into their coffee can, and spoke to them for a moment. Erin watched as they all shook hands. Odd, she thought. He acts as if he knows them.

While Travor soaked up the Louisiana charm, Erin soaked up his. She'd never met such a man. His fascination and appreciation of the struggling artists impressed her, yet she had to wonder at his bleeding-heart attitude. Just like when he wanted to pick up the hitchhiker, or the dogs on the side of the highway; he doled out twenty-dollar bills to all the street performers as if he were made of money. He was so full of enthusiasm—for everything.

He threw his arm around her shoulders. "Now, come on, it's time to find a place to stay."

Her skin sizzled at his touch. Her legs felt so rubbery she could hardly walk beside him. Why on earth did he affect her in such a way? And how could she fight it? She couldn't fight it. And why should she, she wondered. Past, be damned. *I'm a woman now, not a rebellious seventeen-year-old. I don't do things to spite my mother anymore. And I know what precautions to take. I know about love, taking risks . . . what I want.*

She shivered in spite of the August heat. *Past, be damned. . . .*

Erin turned away from the registration desk of the French Market Inn as Travor signed in. He'd told her he didn't want one of those big fancy chain hotels; he wanted something small, intimate, with some Cajun charm and atmosphere.

And this is it, she thought as she ventured down the narrow hall to the courtyard the desk clerk had told them about. She pushed through a door and stepped out onto a brick patio surrounded with delightful greenery. Lawn chairs were sprinkled about, but the courtyard was empty. Erin walked to the center and inhaled. New Orleans had its own special odor. And its own special charm. The City That Care Forgot, she mused. She looked up at the four-story structure with its balconies, and imagined standing on one beneath the stars, in Travor's arms.

She hugged herself. *I want him,* she thought. Not just physically but mentally and emotionally.

All afternoon she'd been shoved against him while meandering through the French Quarter streets. When he'd taken her hand, she'd felt united with her other half. Such a strange feeling for one who'd never had an "other half," she reflected.

Suddenly, he was walking toward her. Anticipation built inside her. God, she'd never felt like this. She'd never so blatantly wanted a man; she was certain he could see it on her face. She didn't care. At this point, all she wanted was to be lost in his arms.

She smiled.

He smiled back.

He stood before her, held out his hand. A key dangled from his fingers.

Her heart pounded harder.

"Your room is right across the hall from mine."

She swayed, unable to believe what she'd heard, yet the words echoed in her ears.

He reached for her. "Hey, you okay?" His arms went around her. The warmth of his skin teased her, taunted her through his T-shirt.

She pulled away. "It...I... It must be all the junk I've eaten—the sugar." She felt the heat rush to her face. She was certain he could read her mind. She was sure she'd just earned an Academy Award for playing the fool. Taking the key, she turned away from him.

"What floor?" she asked, and was stunned to hear an icy coolness lacing the clipped words.

"Second," he answered with just a hint of uncertainty.

Erin punched the elevator button, her mind cursing her naiveté and her overly active imagination. But just because she was a fool was no reason to take it out on Travor. She turned back toward him and forced a smile.

"I— It was a fun afternoon. I suppose we'll be getting up early to get on the road in the morning."

He frowned, concern still evident in his eyes. "It's still early. I thought we'd freshen up, then go out for dinner somewhere, visit a club or two." His lips broke into a smile. "All tourists have to see Pat O'Brien's. It's a world-famous bar with a great piano lounge. It's a tourist rule."

She shook her head. "I'm really tired, Travor. Why don't you go without me?"

He looked disappointed. She felt a twinge of guilt but fiercely fought it away. She couldn't take any more gentle touches, lopsided smiles, seductive winks.

"C'mon," he crooned in that low guttural voice of his. "It wouldn't be the same without you."

She wasn't going to argue. She didn't have the strength. "Call me in an hour." She would turn him down over the telephone; it would be easier that way.

They entered the elevator and didn't speak as they waited to be deposited on the second floor. When the doors opened, they silently walked down the narrow hall. Erin was only vaguely aware that one side of the wall was bricked while the other was papered. She stared down at the carpet. Green with tiny pink flowers.

They reached a dead end.

On their right was room 220. On their left was room 219. A framed print of a solitary magnolia hung from the wall, between the rooms. How appropriate, she mused as they studied the picture. Simultaneously, they turned away from each other.

With her heart racing and a lump in her throat, Erin listened as they each slipped a key into a door. Each turned a key to the right. Two locks clicked. They opened their doors.

"I'll call you," Travor stated, turning to study her face carefully.

Erin nodded and gently closed her door.

Travor paced the floor, shooting condemning glances at the telephone situated beside the bed. He'd given her her hour. He'd called and she had refused. Damn, what had happened? He was certain she'd had a good time. Everything had gone smoothly. Damn, he muttered again, and searched his memory. Had he said something to offend her? Was she wanting to return to Memphis? He ran a shaky hand through his hair. If she wanted him to take her home, he would, but he wouldn't suggest it.

He continued to pace, rerunning their telephone conversation through his mind. She'd been adamant, almost cold.

"I'm tired, Travor. And my head hurts. Can't you find someone else to entertain you?"

Her voice had chilled him to the bone.

Entertain him? *Entertain him?* He wasn't looking for entertainment. He slammed onto the bed, and the mattress springs screeched a protest.

We'll head out tomorrow, bright and early. The sooner I get her to Rattan, the better off we'll be. The country has a way of calming a person down, he thought, and felt a twinge of homesickness. But once again, his mind drifted back to her odd behavior.

It had been when they'd reached the hotel, out in the courtyard, that she'd frozen up. What had shot through her brain? Memories? Was she reacting to something from her past?

Damn, he'd have sworn she was beginning to like him. She hadn't objected to his arm around her, and he had to admit, he'd touched her as much as he could. He'd had the damnedest time keeping his hands off her. Was she just...entertaining him?

He shifted on the bed. She's lucky I didn't follow my instincts, he thought. I could have brought her up here and shown her some "entertainment." I wonder what she'd have thought about that. But he knew.

If I'd gotten one room, it would have pushed her over the edge.

Erin could still feel the wanting, the frustration, the embarrassment. A tear slipped from the corner of her eye and streamed down her cheek. Angrily, she swiped at it.

Serves you right, she thought, stalking back and forth across the carpeted floor. You were ready to jump in the sack at the twitch of that lopsided grin. You were ready to make the same mistakes you made eleven years ago, she accused.

Mistake? No, Kyle Duncan wasn't a mistake. Because she had Max.

Erin stretched out long and stared up at the ceiling. Then, curling on her side, she hugged the pillow. Max is the most important thing in the world to me. And so was his father. Kyle would still be alive if it wasn't for me. If he hadn't been rushing home to marry me ... If I hadn't been pregnant ...

The reality of what she'd done, how she'd acted with Travor danced before her eyes. *How could I have been so foolish? I practically threw myself at him. What must he think?* Her face burned with embarrassment. She pulled the pillow over her head. It smelled lemon-fresh and she vaguely wondered if Travor was propped up against his own pillows.

She fell asleep wondering.

Chapter Seven

Travor maneuvered the van through the darkness. In less than an hour, he would be home. It felt good to be on familiar ground, traveling familiar roads. The thought startled him. He hadn't realized how much he missed East Texas, or the old home place. For so many years, he'd felt trapped there, certain he would never be able to escape. And then he would feel guilty. His mother couldn't help being in bad health. She had no one else; he was her only child, her only living relative. He had to stay home to care for her.

Travor gripped the steering wheel tightly. It hadn't been easy, even with the nursing service. It had been difficult watching her die...slowly, painfully. He shook his head to dispel the memory, and glanced in the rearview mirror.

Erin was asleep in the back of the van. They'd met that morning in the courtyard of the French Market Inn and shared a breakfast buffet. Erin had seemed uncomfortable and there were dark circles beneath her eyes. There were dark circles under his own eyes. He'd tossed and turned the entire night, wondering what he'd said to offend her. This morning, he'd realized Erin had resurrected her doubts about him; she appeared cautious, hesitant with every word she uttered. And her eyes were once again focusing just above his. In spite of her attitude, Travor had insisted they stop in Baton Rouge, tour the Old State Capitol. They didn't get on the road headed for home until late evening. Now he regretted it; he'd been trying to recapture what they'd had in the French Quarter. It hadn't worked.

He frowned. What had happened? He replayed every scene, remembered everything he'd said to her, but still, he couldn't figure it out. He sighed and tried to clear his mind of Erin Weller.

It was just after midnight when he pulled into his drive. He could hardly contain his feeling of excitement as he killed the motor and flicked off the lights. He sat for a moment, half expecting Erin to rise up from the back seat and speak to him. She didn't so he stared out into the darkness, looking at the house he'd grown up in.

While he'd thoroughly enjoyed his time on the road, he had to admit it was damn good to be home, back to what he knew. He liked his friends and neighbors. He'd known them all his life. He liked walking into the grocery store or the bank, and knowing each and every person he met. The one thing that made him uncomfortable while on the road was that no one knew him, no one had said, "Hey-ya, Trav, how's it going today?" No one had acted as if they really cared. Guess I'm just a small-town boy, after all, he mused.

He opened the door as quietly as possible. He didn't want to bring forth a pack of barking dogs and scare Erin. He walked around the van and slid open the door, then eased himself inside. She was curled up in one of the captain's chairs, facing away from him. He put his hand on her shoulder and whispered. "Erin, we're here." She didn't move so he gave her a little shake. She shifted and mumbled.

Travor scooped her into his arms and backed out of the van. She was warm and light. Can't weigh much more than a hundred pounds, he thought. Her head rested against his chest and he could smell that flirty, flowery scent she wore. Moonlight danced in her white-gold hair.

Making his way across the yard, he almost stumbled over a couple of dogs wiggling around his feet.

"Shh," he whispered. "Get back, guys. I'm glad to see you, too, but move on. We'll play tomorrow."

When he opened the door to the house, a pine scent assaulted his nostrils, playing war with Erin's sensuous cologne. He frowned, resenting the intrusive antiseptic smell of the household cleaner. Nellie must have just cleaned that day. Damn if the woman didn't do too much. She'd probably cleaned every day since he'd left—not so much for him, as for the memory of his mother.

"All I wanted was for her to keep an eye on the place and feed the dogs," he mumbled.

He walked across the den and entered the hallway. He hesitated. He wanted to put Erin in his bed. He wanted to feel her next to him, sleep with his arms wrapped around her. He reined in his thoughts and entered the smaller bedroom. Awkwardly, he tugged back the covers, placed her on the stark-white sheets, then stood staring down at her. Should he loosen her clothing, unbutton the tight jeans she was wearing? He decided against it. He slipped off her shoes and dropped them to the floor. He pulled a comforter up to her waist.

Damn, I'm crazy for not crawling in beside her. I was a fool for not getting one room last night in New Orleans.

She looked like such a woman-child. So sweet and innocent, yet so damned sexy. He exhaled and shook his head. He wondered if bringing her home with him was such a good idea.

Erin opened her eyes and stared at the ceiling. Then she surveyed the unfamiliar room with the antique dresser and matching chifforobe. A round table stood beside the bed. She sat up and rubbed her face.

Her clothing was wrinkled; she was wearing exactly what she'd had on the day before. And then morning sounds began to filter through her foggy, confused brain.

Birds chirped. An owl hooted. Dogs barked. There must be a kennel nearby, she thought. She jumped out of bed and crossed the small room to the window. She pulled back curtains that matched the bedspread, and peered out. Cows. Hills. Pastureland. Pine trees. An unpaved road in front of the house.

A tremulous exhilaration raced through her. Everything seemed so bright and new.

Erin crossed the room again and opened the door. No sounds came from inside the house. Running a hand through her disheveled hair, she tiptoed along the hall and entered a large living area. A stone fireplace dominated the far side of the wall. A rag rug covered the floor. The room had an earthy lived-in look and Erin liked it immediately. She made her way through, touching inanimate objects as if she were dreaming, and entered what was obviously the kitchen. A long pine picnic table claimed her attention. She touched it.

She gazed at the cupboards filled with pottery and glassware. The doors were lined with what looked like chicken wire. She'd never tried to imagine what kind of house Travor might live in, but this would have been beyond her fantasies. It was a far cry from the Presley decor in Lou's house.

Much to Lou's chagrin, Erin's favorite pastime was browsing through decorating magazines, daydreaming. She even cut out favorite pictures, keeping them in a photo album—just in case she ever had a home of her own.

And this is a home, she thought, running both hands along the cool, yellow-topped counter. I wouldn't change a thing.

Erin heard a shout from outside and moved toward French doors. She peered across an expansive white-cedar deck toward trees and a barn. Her mouth dropped open. Travor had one foot in a tire swing and was swaying back and forth with a pack of dogs chasing after him. It was the most delightful sight she had ever seen: a grown man playing that way.

She slapped a hand over her mouth to stifle a giggle bubbling in her throat. Suddenly, several of the dogs pricked their ears and turned toward her. They raced across the yard, up on the deck and stood on hind legs. They barked, whined, and bared their teeth. Erin was certain one of them was smiling at her. She backed up and placed a hand over her heart, eyeing the pads of their paws pressed against the glass. She'd never owned a dog.

"Good morning," Travor called and leaped from the tire swing. He jogged to the double doors. "Back, Rachel...get down, Harry!" He peered in at Erin and grinned. "I forgot to tell you about them." He waved an arm to indicate the animals. "You don't have anything against dogs, do you?"

Taken aback by his appearance, Erin didn't answer. He was wearing running gear. His black shorts were cut high. His teal-colored T-shirt clung to his chest and his skin glistened with perspiration. With a conscious effort, she lifted her eyes to meet his.

He grinned at her as if he could read her thoughts. He leaned against the door and pointed toward the counter. "There's coffee. Just made it about half an hour ago. Bring a cup out here." He motioned to the deck with its table and chairs.

Erin shook her head. "No way. I'm not coming out there. Those guys look hungry." She looked at the dogs; there must have been a dozen of them in all shapes and sizes.

Travor threw back his head and laughed. The sound of it sent tingly sensations all through Erin. He seemed so different here he even looked different.

She ran a hand through her hair, suddenly aware of how she must look. She smiled at him. "Give me a few minutes, then we'll discuss where I drink my coffee."

Travor took her arm and they walked out onto the multilevel deck that ran the length of the house. "Just stay calm. They'll sniff, but they won't hurt you."

In spite of Travor's reassurance, Erin's quick cup of coffee churned in her stomach and she flung herself against his body, almost climbing the length of him when the pack of dogs came running toward them.

Travor laughed and swung her easily into his arms. "Thanks, guys," he called to his many animals. "I knew you were good for something."

Erin hit him teasingly against the chest. Her actions surprised her. She didn't want to act coy or flirtatious. And she didn't want to get too comfortable in Travor's arms, his home or his life.

"Where do you find all these animals?" she asked, trying to center his attention on something other than her.

Travor walked toward the tire swing, carrying her easily. "People drop them off. We don't have a humane society or a pound here in Rattan. The nearest one's twenty miles away."

"I can't imagine why you keep them."

"My mother started this, years ago. It was kind of a hobby. She loved animals. When she died, I just kept doing it."

Erin reached out for the tire swing and pulled it to her. Travor helped her stand on it, but hung on to the rope. She shook her head. "We never had any pets. Lou is allergic to cats, and she always told us dogs were too much trouble.

"They are trouble—if you take care of them right. I get them checked out by the vet, given their shots, neutered or spayed. You'd be surprised how many I give away. People come from all around when they need a pet for a special occasion. It's hard, though."

"I'll bet it is. Feeding them. Lugging them back and forth to the vet. And the expense of it all."

Travor looked surprised. "That's the easy part. The hard part is giving them away. I get attached."

She laughed. "Why didn't I know that?"

Travor looked at his canine friends. They were gathered around, some sitting on their haunches, watching as if Erin and Travor were performing for them.

Suddenly, Travor pulled the tire swing taut, then leaped up beside her as it sailed through the air. Erin shrieked and the dogs became excited and chased after them. They barked and jumped and nipped.

"Travor, not so high! This is crazy!" She held tightly to the rope and tried to keep her balance. Her eyes never left the dogs. They were obviously enjoying the game much more than she was. She suspected they viewed her tender flesh as their reward.

"You're supposed to yell 'Higher, higher.' Don't you remember when you were a kid and wanted to touch the sky?" He pushed again.

Erin gritted her teeth. "The limb is going to break— it's creaking—" She threw her leg over the tire, straddling it the way Travor was doing. As a result, they were thigh to thigh. His legs were hot; she could feel the heat of them through her thin slacks but there was nothing she could do about it. His hands grasped the rope just below hers. Her breast pressed against his knuckles. The proximity of his body so close to hers, the heat of him almost caused her to let go, take her chances with the animals below. She didn't know who was more dangerous: Travor Steele or all those dogs.

"Travor—"

"Don't worry," he said, looking up at the limb. "This old tree was around when I was a kid. You're safe."

Erin looked up. The tree was monstrous; the limb looked thick and strong. Patches of blue sky peeked through the branches as if to reassure her nothing bad could ever happen in Rattan, Texas. Especially not in Travor Steele's backyard. And she believed it.

As the tire came to a lazy stop, Travor leaped to the ground and reached up for Erin. She hesitated before putting her hands on his shoulders. As she'd suspected, he felt strong, solid through his T-shirt. His muscles rippled hot beneath her fingers. His hands gripped her waist and he brought her down slowly, directly against the front of him. On purpose? she wondered.

As his head dipped toward hers, she sniffed the arresting scent of his after-shave, mingled with male perspiration and fresh country air. Raising her face, she anticipated the touch, the taste of his lips. His hands readjusted from her waist, moving upward to the sides of her breasts. They seared her skin through her cotton blouse. Erin stepped closer to him, lips parted, ready to receive what she ached for...and a cackle from the side of the house pierced the air.

"Merciful heavens! Lord of the Earth! Look who's decided to come home!"

Erin jerked away from Travor, struggling desperately to get control of her emotions. As she straightened her blouse that had been worked out of her slacks, she knew beyond a shadow of doubt that desire must be written all over her face. And she knew immediately— before Travor called her name—that the short plump lady approaching them was Nellie. So much for the tiny birdlike woman she'd imagined. She vividly recollected Nellie's loose tongue.

God, I hope I don't look like I've romped around in that barn, she thought.

Travor walked over to Nellie, looped his arm around her broad shoulders.

The woman poked him in the ribs. "Well, cat got your tongue? Introduce me, Travor Lee. I s'pose this here's the owner of that fancy set of wheels in your dirt drive. Them Tennessee plates what got my attention. You got a call from Tennessee just a—"

Erin leaped forward. "Hello, I'm Erin Weller. And your name?" She was vaguely aware of Travor quirking one eyebrow at her but she kept her gaze on Nellie. The woman tried out a number of facial expressions before settling on one that plainly stated she knew it was Erin who had called.

The older woman reached for Erin's hand. "I'm Nellie from across the pasture. I been caring for Travor Lee's pack of hounds while he was away, but I 'spect you know that."

Erin felt her face go hot. The woman was obviously going to torment her with little digs. And Travor was eyeing them both questioningly.

"You answered a call from Tennessee, Nellie?" he asked.

"Sure did. 'Course, the caller didn't say she was from there. But I seen on some of them TV shows that you could call the operator and check where a call is from, so that's what I done."

Both of them turned their gazes to Erin, who could feel her face color once again.

Travor frowned. "It must have been Lou. You'll have to call her back."

Nellie frowned, too, and eyed Erin.

Erin didn't say a word. She didn't want Travor to know she'd called to check up on him—not that it mattered now. He would understand that it was the logical thing for her to do. Wouldn't he? I'll tell him later, she thought. Not in front of this woman. She pushed the call from her mind.

"How long you staying?" Nellie asked. Before Erin could answer, she turned to Travor. "Your mother wouldn't hold to a young woman staying overnight with you—alone, no chaperons around. Remember what she always said, Travor Lee. When you lose your good reputation, then you've not got much left."

Travor laughed and hugged the woman. "You're a prize, Nellie. But this is the nineties. Besides, this is business."

Business? She'd almost forgotten. Still, Erin felt the sting of the word. Was it business when he took her in his arms and almost kissed her?

"What kind of business?" Nellie asked, somewhat suspiciously, Erin thought.

They both looked at Travor for his answer.

He grinned. "Monkey business," he whispered and winked at Erin. The sting of his previous comment dissipated into a floating bubble of anticipation. She grinned back.

"You kid around all you want, Travor Lee Steele, but you just wait. When old Mrs. Lucas finds out you got a woman staying with you, she's gonna call up Reverend Perkins and he's gonna come callin' and then—"

Travor maneuvered Nellie around and was heading back to the front of the house, but Erin could hear the woman's words loud and clear. She had to agree with Nellie. A town as small as Rattan? Yes, she was going to be big news.

When Travor offered to give Erin a tour of his house, she knew she should steer them into a working mode. They had so much to do. But she didn't. She couldn't.

She wasn't ready to immerse him in "Elvis." She wanted to enjoy Travor before he became someone else. Here in this country atmosphere, everything was different, including Travor—but especially her. And she liked the feeling.

Travor proudly escorted her through the rooms, explaining how he'd knocked out walls and windows to make the place spacious, bright and comfortable. Erin marveled at his plans for a bedroom that wasn't quite finished. With its wall of shelves, it would be perfect for Max, she mused, then pushed the thought from her mind.

She was totally captivated by Travor's own sexy bedroom just across the hall from where she'd slept. It had been added on to the house before he'd built the deck and purposely portrayed the feeling of openness, nature and space. He'd incorporated the deck with the room and as in the kitchen, French doors were utilized, separating the sleeping area from the outdoor social area. Lightweight, gauzy curtains covered the windows but in no way hindered sunlight or offered privacy. Opposite the king-size bed, Travor had built a platform that ran the width of the room. Beneath it, a winter store of dry, well-seasoned wood waited to be used. In the center of the platform, situated on a slab of slate, a Franklin stove rested between two windows.

Erin's heart flip-flopped when Travor pointed out the shower he'd installed on the deck. She could just imagine standing beside him, naked, beneath a spray of hot water and a midnight sky full of stars.

By the time they'd finished their tour, Erin was feeling much the same as she had in New Orleans. His little-boy smile teased at her heart. His eyes hypnotized her; she felt absorbed into his being. She wanted him to take her in his arms and press her solidly to him. She longed for him to touch her. And she wanted more, much more than that. She felt as though she could live in this house forever.

"Well, it's almost noon. Do you want to eat lunch or do you want to play Elvis?" Travor asked.

Erin blinked away her fantasy, very much aware that Travor wasn't sharing the same feelings. She moved toward the television and yanked up the satchel that Lou had packed with Elvis tapes and books.

"You'd better start doing your homework. Try to develop that 'edge' over all the others. Elvis impersonators are a dime a dozen." When she realized how testy her voice sounded, she shrugged, embarrassed. She was glad Travor didn't comment about her odd behavior.

With one hand, he rummaged in the satchel and brought out, ironically, the *King Creole* tape, reminding Erin of their stay in New Orleans.

She reached for it. "Let's start with something else, maybe a documentary so you can get a feel for his life."

"No, I want to watch this one. You got real excited about it down in New Orleans. I want to know why."

She yanked it away from him. "A documentary will better prepare you...then you'll understand why." Pure prattle, she thought. *King Creole* would only remind her of how badly she'd wanted him in New Orleans, how foolishly she'd acted.

How foolish I *am* acting, she corrected. But in spite of her foolishness, Erin couldn't remember ever having as much fun as she'd had—was still having—with Travor. It was like starting over, starting fresh and new. Being given a second chance. She felt a lump building in her throat. Was she being unfair? Was she betraying Kyle's memory? If she fell in love with another man, did

it mean Kyle had died in vain—on his way to marry her
and give their child his name? But I'm not falling in
love, Erin told herself, and shook her guilt away.

Travor punched in a tape and moved back to the sofa.
Someone had neglected to rewind that particular movie
from the last time it was viewed, and Erin smiled when
Travor cocked an eyebrow at her, then pressed the Rewind button.

"Sorry, we're not very good at rewinding at our
house."

"All it takes is a flick of the finger. A bad habit...a
really bad habit to get into. You know, if the video
stores would enforce the rule—"

"Just play the tape," she instructed and tried to get
the remote control out of his hand.

He pulled away from her. "Oh, no, you don't." He
aimed it at the big screen and clicked. Soon, a young
Elvis appeared on the screen, singing and shaking to
"That's Alright, Mama."

"Damn," Travor mumbled. "Ya'll want me to do
that?"

Erin giggled.

Travor swore again and made a face. Then he froze.
"My God," he murmured, "it's Lou."

The image of the young blond-haired girl standing so
still, staring up at her idol, always sent chills coursing
up and down Erin's spine. "She really hasn't changed
much, has she? She was thirteen then."

Travor looked at her, astonished. "Just a kid."

Erin nodded. "See that brown-haired girl on Lou's
left? That's her older sister. She took Lou to that
show—her first time to ever see Elvis."

"And she was hooked, wasn't she? It's obvious."
Travor rewound the tape again. He couldn't believe

what he was seeing. A young Lou Weller standing amid hundreds of screaming fans. But Lou wasn't screaming. There were no tears on her cheeks. Her arms weren't outstretched. She looked as if she were seeing God Himself. Her face was glowing, even though the film was black-and-white, Travor could tell she was glowing. She was hooked, all right. She loved him. It was so damned obvious. Travor felt something building in his throat, behind his eyes. Damn, if he wasn't careful, he'd be bursting into tears. He blinked, rewound the tape again. He wanted to see her once more.

Erin watched the clip again, as she had so many times. "She looks sweet, doesn't she?"

"Yeah," he agreed. "What about her sister? I didn't realize she had other family."

Erin shrugged even though Travor wasn't looking at her. Like him, she couldn't take her eyes off the screen. "Abbie was killed in a car wreck not long after that. Lou worshiped Abbie." Erin felt that too-familiar lump form in her throat. She couldn't help but wonder what Lou would have become had Abbie lived. Would their lives have been different? She forced the thought away. "I guess Lou went a little wild after that. She hung out on the Presleys' front lawn with a lot of other girls, and tried every way she could to be near Elvis. But his mother—Mrs. Presley—would come out and talk to the kids and tell them to go on back home, that she wouldn't introduce them to her son if they were skipping school or runaways. She and Lou became friends. Lou left home the day she graduated from high school and headed out to California. Because they'd known each other in Memphis, she was hired as an extra in several of his movies. She always found a way to get what she wanted."

Travor shook his head, trying to picture Lou negoti- ating with Mrs. Presley just to meet her son. Or deal- ing with some of the movie moguls. He remembered the women who'd chased him across the parking lot in Memphis. "Women would do anything for him, wouldn't they? And after all these years, he still affects them the same way."

"It's something, isn't it? To be loved like that. To be worshiped."

"Would you want to be worshiped?" he asked.

She shrugged. "I don't know. It might be nice."

"Would you want to be loved like that?"

The tone of his voice, low and raspy, sent a mixture of fear and wonder through her. Heat consumed her body. "It might be kind of scary."

"In what way?"

She shrugged again. "I just can't imagine that kind of love."

"I guess I can't, either."

Erin looked at him. "And how could one ever return it?"

"Like this." Before she realized what he was doing, Travor pulled her into his arms and buried his face in the top of her hair. Chills stole across her body as she relaxed against him.

Lifting her chin, Travor looked into her face. He groaned and his lips came down on hers so gently, so sweetly, that she wondered why she had been fighting her feelings. It was time to let go of the past. It was time to love again.

Then his hands were unbuttoning her blouse, slip- ping her bra straps off her shoulders while simulta- neously, he eased down on the sofa and pulled her on top of him.

Travor wrapped her in his arms and kneaded the small of her back, letting his hands move up and down, pressing, caressing. He savored the warmth of her, and how she snuggled into him. He inhaled the gentle fragrance of her hair and wanted to bury his face in it once again. Should he make love to her? Damn, why did he have to think? Why couldn't he just act? Because he didn't take making love lightly and because he didn't want to be hurt, to be made a fool of. He knew instinctively that Erin could destroy him. She was just the kind of woman he could fall for, one who could smash his heart into a billion tiny pieces. He couldn't let that happen. And he wouldn't.

Desire throbbed deep inside her. She wanted him. She didn't want to think anymore, or wonder what if... God, why couldn't she get the past out of her mind? Concentrate on "now." Now might be all they had.

His distinct, clean woodsy after-shave clung to him, tantalizing her senses, just as his hands did as they worked their way lower, down her hips. She pressed against him, willing him to undress her.

But he didn't. Instead, his hands froze and he tried to sit up on the sofa. "We can't do this, Erin."

She clung to him, swallowed. "Why not? If I'm willing, why the hell not?"

Her anger startled him. He moved her off him and straightened. "I'm sorry. It's just that—" He shrugged. "I'm sorry."

Anger consumed her. Frustration burned through her chest. "No, you aren't, Travor. You're not sorry, you're scared."

"God, don't do this. Don't make it any tougher."

"You're the one making it tough. Don't you see what you're doing? Don't you see what the problem is?"

"No, I don't. What is the problem, Erin?" He turned away from her, ran a hand through his hair, tried to get a grip on his emotions and the sarcasm in his voice.

"It's Celeste."

He jerked around. Where the hell had she heard about Celeste? They hadn't left the house; she hadn't met anyone from Rattan, except . . .

Erin swallowed. "When we were in Memphis . . ."

He quirked an eyebrow.

She shrugged, knowing it was time to explain. "I checked you out. You said you lived in Rattan, Texas, so I called Information and dialed your number. Nellie was at your house . . . cleaning, I suppose." She shrugged again, hoping he would understand, that she wasn't making things worse. "All I wanted to know was if you were really who you said you were. I'm sorry, Travor."

He reached over to touch her but changed his mind, as if he knew that any kind of physical contact would spark the embers that smoldered in each of them. "You should have checked me out. You were damn trusting to even let me stay the night."

"That wasn't my idea, if you remember."

"Thank God for adventurous eleven-year-old boys. . . ." He paused before adding, "And Elvis lovers, I guess."

"Travor, about Celeste . . ."

A frown flickered across his face. Erin hesitated, toyed with her fingers, then glanced at him nervously, wondering if she'd said too much. She sensed that he didn't want to talk about Celeste. Neither did she, but she had to know: was he still in love with her? "Well?"

"Well, what?" he asked.

"Well, Celeste. That's what. Don't you want to tell me the rest of the story?"

Travor let out a breath he was holding, then leaned back in the sofa. He pursed his lips, as if deep in thought, remembering. Then he cleared his throat and began.

"I was so grossly overweight, and flattered as hell at the attention Celeste showed me. Guess I went overboard returning that attention. She was a single mother trying desperately to make ends meet, and I was just damned stupid. I was willing to marry her, take on the responsibility of raising her fatherless kid. The worst part is—I honestly believed she liked me and I ran out and bought a four-carat diamond." He held up his hand to show her the ring. "We set the date, invited the entire town but guess what? The bride never made it to the wedding."

Erin could tell Travor was embarrassed by the experience. Embarrassed that she knew. "I'm sorry, Travor. I didn't mean to pry. Nellie really told me more than I wanted to know."

"That's okay. Celeste did me a big favor. What if I'd married her? I'd be living right here in Rattan, Texas, raising her kids and working for a living." He shook his head and flexed his long fingers. "I learned a lesson. A very valuable lesson."

When it seemed as if he wasn't going to explain, Erin asked, "What, Travor?"

He looked at her, his eyes cold and hard. "No one will ever make a fool of me again." Then he smiled, and reached out to run a forefinger across her cheek. "Not even you."

Chapter Eight

He's acting like a jerk, she thought, sitting on the deck, waiting for Travor to join her. Ever since their heart-to-heart about Celeste, Travor had been acting cocky. He'd brag about his oil wells, flirt outrageously using sexual innuendo, and he seemed to strut. Erin wasn't sure what had brought on this new personality. Was he sorry he'd told her he'd been stood-up at the altar? Was he trying to make Erin pay for what Celeste did to him? That same evening, Travor had surprised them both by telling Erin about his dad dying and his mother's illness. And how afraid he'd been. He had told her he tried not to think of it anymore, and that he'd certainly never shared such intimate secrets and feelings. Erin had listened carefully and caringly, never interrupting.

"It was tough being overweight. And as hard as it was for me, I know it's got to be ten times harder for a girl than a guy," he'd confessed.

Travor had told her about his lonely childhood. How he'd been too heavy for sports, and too shy to get involved in school activities. "That's the reason I learned to do impersonations—for entertainment." And how, when his dad died, his mother had put him in charge of things, told him he was the man of the house. He'd taken his position seriously. He told Erin how he and his mother had argued when he'd refused to sell the little electrical company his father had started, and against his mother's wishes, he had quit school to run it. There had been tears in his voice when he told how they'd plodded along, barely making ends meet. Then they'd learned that Dorothy Steele had cancer and that it was just a matter of time for her. They couldn't afford to keep her in a hospital or hire private nurses, so Travor ran the business from their home and took care of his mother. He rarely left her alone, except with very good friends like Nellie. When Dorothy Steele died, he sold the business and invested every cent in an oil well. Then he'd prayed to high heaven that it wasn't a dry hole.

Erin looked around the multilevel deck. Evidently, his prayers had been answered.

"I always wanted to play the guitar," Travor said, swaggering through the French doors. His blue shirt was unbuttoned and Erin could see his thick chest hair peeking through. He sat down in a deck chair and propped Lou's old Washburn on his knee. He began strumming the four chords Erin had taught him. C—strum, strum. G—strum, strum. A—strum, strum. D—strum, strum. Looking up at her, he grinned.

"You're a natural," she complimented. "It almost seems like everything you touch turns to—"

"Gold? Oil?" He rolled his shoulders and Erin recognized that he was shifting into an impersonation.

"How about stardust?" she asked and made a face.

"Well, imagine that. I'm a golden boy," he said, in a most authentic Elvis voice. "Wonder when that happened."

Erin rolled her eyes and shook her head. He'd sounded just like the ex-con, Vince Everett, in *Jailhouse Rock*. "Just remember, everyone has their moment of glory. It can end as quickly as it begins."

"I never sweat the small stuff," he quipped, strumming away.

Ever since their close call on the sofa, Travor insisted on getting to work, developing his Elvis persona. That suited Erin, but his cocky new attitude didn't. He appeared to have opted for that arrogant, chip-on-the-shoulder style, and Erin found it annoying. On top of that, he acted as if nothing had happened between them. He still flirted and teased, and there were a lot of winks and touches, but they didn't seem to mean anything—not like before. It was as if he was purposely tormenting her. Getting back at Celeste? Erin wondered. Or is this the real Travor Steele?

Damn those winks! And damn that cocky attitude.

They would rise each morning from their separate beds and have breakfast, then Travor would go out to jog. When he returned and showered, they'd watch Elvis movies. There were times when Travor would retreat to his office in another part of the house to take care of business, and he'd be on the phone for an hour or more. For the past four days they had cooked together, eaten together, worked together—and Erin realized she loved every minute of it.

As she sat and watched him practice the four chords, Erin admitted to herself just how much she enjoyed looking at him, being near him. The very sight of him made her heart pound in her chest. How could he affect her in such a way? Why hadn't Kyle? She didn't understand any of it, and if the truth were known, she didn't want to. She just wanted to enjoy it.

"Earth to Erin... Earth to Erin. Come in, please."

Erin realized Travor was speaking to her.

"What were you daydreaming about? Imagining me onstage in front of the masses?" He shot her an arrogant little grin.

"I don't think you're quite ready for the masses."

"Oh, you don't, do you? Well, watch this." He stood, spread his legs apart, shoved the guitar under his left arm and quivered with all his might. Erin burst into giggles.

"Okay, baby...what'll it be? 'Jailhouse Rock' or 'Hot Dog'? 'Don't Be Cruel' or 'Guitar Man'? I'm ready for the big time." He quivered again.

Erin stood. "Please, please. No more." She moved toward him. "You'll have to do more than just quiver. Use your arms. And don't forget to cue your band to let them know where you're going with each movement. Haven't you noticed how Elvis kept his fingers and hands unclenched, open? And use your legs...like this." She demonstrated, spreading her arms and jerking her shoulders. Then she bent her left leg toward her right one and quickly heel-toed across the deck.

"Hey, not bad. Let's have a little music." Travor flipped a switch on the wall, and "Whole Lot-ta Shakin' Goin' On" boomed through the speakers. Travor copied Erin's heel-toe action, awkwardly.

"That needs some work," Erin said. "Try this. It goes with the quiver." She placed all her weight on the balls of her feet and then she gracefully jerked herself across the floor.

"How'd you do that?" he asked, trying to emulate her frenzied movements.

"Do this," she shouted above the music. Her legs appeared to have a life of their own, her shoulders twitched and her hips swayed with wild abandon. Travor stopped to watch, pounding the back of the guitar in time with Erin and the music.

"You're too good," he shouted. "I can't do that."

"You'd better. We're sinking a lot of money into you." She took the guitar away from him and set it aside. "Use your arms. Elvis used every inch of his body." She ran her hands down the front of him, hooking her fingers in the waistband of his jeans. Suddenly, all she wanted was to make him aware of her. To make him feel the need, the desire, the frustration she was feeling.

Travor tried to back away from her, but she had a death grip. "Move that middle. Come on, gyrate." She pulled and pushed, causing his hips to bump against her. "Loosen up, try it again. Listen to the music," she ordered, pushing, pulling on his midsection.

"Concentrate. Close your eyes and think Elvis. Move your legs, your hips, your shoulders and arms. Every inch of your skin is feeling the music."

No, he thought. *Every inch of my skin is feeling you.*

She ran her hands over his shoulders, then she stepped back and let her eyes slowly move down the length of him. She frowned. "Something's not right here."

"What?" he asked, looking down at his open shirt.

"Of course . . ." She smiled, inching toward him.

Travor backed away from her but not quickly enough. She gripped his belt loop and pulled him toward her. Then she reached up with her right hand and touched his chest. "You remember— Elvis didn't have a hairy chest."

"Yeah, well, I'm not Elvis."

"But everything has to be authentic.... Lou likes it that way. Besides, no self-respecting Elvis impersonator would dare make such a blunder."

"Well, I would, and Lou can just..."

Moving closer, she crooned, "So...shall I shave it?"

"No way—"

She massaged his chest, just below his right shoulder. "Or we could use hot wax?"

He was backed against the wall of the house. "Cut it out, Erin. This is crazy."

But Erin couldn't cut it out. She knew better in her mind, and in her heart, but she felt out of control. She pulled on a sad expression as she ran an open palm across his chest. "I'm afraid it'll have to go, Travor. Everything's riding on this." Suddenly, she grabbed a fistful and Travor flinched. Then she opened her hand and ran it slowly, seductively across his chest. "It won't hurt," she promised between dry lips.

"And damn it, neither will this," he whispered. He scooped her up in one quick, easy movement and carried her toward the hammock on the other side of the deck. He laid her in the springy, mesh material and leaned across her. Then he covered her mouth with his.

Now Elvis was singing "Loving Arms" and Erin was cursing herself for her own stupidity. All she'd wanted to do was tease him—okay, torment him. Just the way he'd been tormenting her. She hadn't planned for it to backfire. She hadn't planned to feel anything. But she did feel something. And it was all she could do to keep from wrapping her arms around him, pulling him closer, pressing against him. She wanted to let him know that she wanted him; now, yesterday, immediately if not sooner. But she fought against her traitorous feelings; she couldn't—not again. She wouldn't let him reject her again. She struggled against him, but her entire body reacted to his kiss. And Travor knew it.

His hands moved to the front of her blouse. She heard a tear, buttons popped and the sounds punctuated the rhythmic throbbing between her legs. Her desire buoyed to an unbearable state.

"I want you, Erin. Now," he whispered against her mouth.

He wanted her! She answered with a kiss so filled with desire that she was certain she must have bitten him. She heard him, felt him moan against her lips.

The hammock rocked wildly, dangerously close to bucking them onto the deck. It wouldn't have mattered; only added to the fury of their passion.

She lifted herself slightly so that he could unhook her bra, but he didn't bother. He shoved it up and palmed both breasts. His hands kneaded, sculpted, his touch pure torture. His thumbs brushed over peaked nipples. His mouth left a hot trail of kisses across her neck and down her chest. Then slowly, seductively, he took one peaked bud into his mouth, and Erin's body convulsed wildly; she cried out.

Surprised, Travor looked up at her and saw tears on her flushed cheeks.

"God, Erin, how long has it been?"

Fresh tears pooled in her eyes. "I haven't made love to anyone...since...since Max's father," she whispered.

She hadn't made love to anyone in eleven years. *Eleven years!*

The words turned his blood to ice. He wanted to run like hell away from her, but at the same time, he wanted to cling more tightly. But he didn't, he couldn't. Filled with regret, he gently released her.

"I can't—I shouldn't have—" He shrugged, unable to say the words in his mind. "I'm sorry, Erin."

He fumbled with her blouse before he remembered that he'd ripped it apart. A button hung by a single thread.

"I'm not sorry," she whispered. The tears ran down her face. He shook his head and backed away from her.

Pulling her torn shirt tightly to her limp body, Erin watched as he disappeared around the corner of the house. Why couldn't he fall in love with her?

Travor had lost the battle and he knew it. And he was very close to losing the war.

A quiver of fear raced through his veins. He'd been making love to Erin Weller constantly in his head from the moment he'd met her. He knew precisely how to touch her, where to touch her. And he knew exactly how her skin would taste.

But you're all talk, Steele, he chastised himself. No matter how badly he wanted to make love to Erin, he wouldn't. It was too much of a risk. He never wanted to be hurt again. He never wanted to be the talk of the town again.

He'd never forget how it had felt when he'd learned Celeste had left town with another man, while he and the entire population of Rattan, Texas—and then some—were at the church waiting for her. What a fool he'd been. And what was worse, he'd been warned. Nellie had never liked Celeste. Travor told himself that Nellie was critical of everybody. But Herm had warned him that Celeste flirted with every guy who came through the Chicken Hut. Travor hadn't cared. He wanted a woman who liked people, could make friends easily, was outgoing. He had told Herm he liked the way Celeste carried on with the customers. Yeah, he'd been a fool. A first-class fool.

But Erin is different. She's not that way. She's quiet and private, and serious.

And she hasn't made love in a long time. The very thought of getting involved with her scared him. She would need and expect so much from him. He wasn't sure he could give it. Not yet. Not now. He ran a hand through his hair, hating the confusion he felt, and the fear.

Damn, if only there were rules to follow. Travor knew without a doubt, that the old saying, ''All's fair in love and war,'' was true. And that the best way not to get hurt, was not to play the game.

If I concentrate on keeping my distance—if I just forget about how sweet she smells, how her skin tastes between my lips—I'll be okay. But God, if she looks at me with that mischievous little twinkle in her eyes, and that playful smile, I won't be able to resist.

She'd looked so sexy dancing across the deck in her tight jeans and that denim shirt tied at the waist. It had been all he could do to keep from carrying her into the bedroom. Damn, he hadn't even thought of a bed. He'd been ready to take her right there in the hammock. And when she'd teased him about shaving his chest, raked her hands across his chest, scratching with her fingernails, gently, teasingly tugging...

He ran a hand across his face and moaned deep down in his gut. Because he knew he couldn't resist her. And he knew the moment he made love to her, he'd be lost. He'd be her fool.

It was five o'clock in the morning. Erin awoke abruptly and squirmed beneath the sheets. Travor's sheets on Travor's bed. She knew she shouldn't have, but when he didn't return last night she'd moved into his room...just to feel near him. She'd finally fallen asleep, wrapped in the clean woodsy scent of the room and the lingering smell of his after-shave. She knew he wouldn't return last night; he was trying to figure things out. And until he did, he wouldn't be coming around her.

She heard a vehicle pull into the driveway. Stunned, she held her breath and listened. Silence. A car door slammed. Was it Travor? Get back to your own room, she ordered, but she couldn't move. She waited, little tingling sensations dancing across her naked skin.

The front door didn't open.

She jumped when she heard footsteps crossing the deck. They came closer and she looked across the room at the French doors. She couldn't leave now. He would see her. Yet she knew she shouldn't stay. What would he do if he found her there? Take her into his arms, love her? She was being an idiot. How many times did he have to reject her before she got the message? She rose to her knees, pulled the sheet tightly around her, then she froze.

There he was, a silhouette against the sheer curtains. He tossed a newspaper and some mail onto a chair, then he unbuttoned his shirt, unzipped his jeans. He used one foot to pry off one of the high rubber boots he wore, then bent and yanked off the other one. Dressed like that, he must have been at the well site. He tugged his faded jeans from his hips. The gauzy curtains provided him with little privacy and Erin fought away the Peeping-Tom feeling consuming her.

She listened to the water running, and imagined him rubbing his large hand across his hairy chest. She stifled the urge to join him in the shower. She could barely keep from squirming.

Now's your chance to get the hell out of here, she told herself. Still, she didn't move. It was time for them to talk, to get things out in the open. She would tell him she loved him. She was sure of that now, if nothing else. Then they would make love. And this time she wouldn't let him run away.

The pelting sound of water ceased. In her mind, Erin pictured Travor reaching for a towel, rubbing it against his wet skin. Then the shower door opened and she watched as he moved tiredly across the deck, drying himself as he went. He wrapped the towel around his waist and opened the French doors.

Erin didn't breathe, but watched as he turned to retrieve the collection of papers. He opened the front page, and Erin saw his entire body react.

"Damn!" he muttered. "Damn it all to hell!" He moved angrily into the room toward the bedside lamp and flicked it on.

Erin stiffened, pulling the sheet tighter around her. "What is it? What's wrong?"

Travor looked surprised, but it quickly changed back to anger. His eyes glinted with a touch of fire as he tossed the newsprint toward her. "See for yourself."

Not knowing what to expect, Erin looked down at the newspaper. She gasped. Sprawled across the front page, the headline blared, A Real Comeback For The King! Beneath it, a large picture of Elvis Presley at his heaviest demanded attention. Then, a series of smaller pix showed Travor in a variety of poses. In one, he was dressed in black leather, flanked by bodyguards. Another showed him entering Star Music Studio while several portrayed him in action shots with Erin in New Orleans. The last picture caught her looking right at the camera, as if signaling the photographer. Her heart battered her breastbone; her ears rang as a throbbing started in her head. Her stomach roiled as she looked up and met Travor's hostile eyes.

"Pretty good publicity stunt. Wish I'd known about it."

"Oh, Lou—" she began, but Travor slammed the mail down on the bedside table, interrupting her.

"You can't blame this one on Lou," he accused.

Erin looked up incredulously. "But it *was* Lou. Can't you see—"

"Yeah, I see. I see you looking straight at the photographer. You knew he was there, you signaled him— look at your hand. Look at that conniving little grin around your lips." He paced the floor angrily, then stopped. "And I'm just sitting there beside you—playing the fool! There's no way you can deny that."

A feeling of helplessness swamped her. She didn't understand why he was so angry, and why he didn't expect publicity. "Travor, I swear. I wouldn't do this without talking it over with you. I'd never go this far—"

He smirked, eyeing her from head to toe. "Looks to me like you're willing to go as far as it takes to get what you want—to save your little studio."

Erin felt heat consume her inside and out. She jumped out of bed, taking the sheet with her, holding it tightly against her. "How dare you suggest such a thing. I'm not that way and you know it."

"I don't know a thing about you," he sneered. "You pick me up in a parking lot. You let me spend the night in your house. You come all the way to Texas with me and—"

"You're twisting everything."

"Just the way you probably twisted that story." He yanked the paper away from her and scanned it. "There's a promise of more to come. What kind of things do you plan for the next edition, Erin? Have there been any photographers lurking around in my backyard?"

Erin moved toward the door. "For the last time, Travor, I didn't know anything about this."

He stiffened his back and looked at her through cold, narrowed eyes; then they glazed over with an arrogant, who-gives-a-damn look that Erin had never seen before.

"I should have listened to my gut feelings. I should have known it was just a matter of time. Dammit all to hell, Erin. When people see this God-awful picture—" He paused, then continued between clenched teeth, "You're the last woman who will ever make a fool of me."

She jutted out her chin and assumed her own who-gives-a-damn-look. She made her voice flippant. "Oh, Travor, give it a rest. Publicity goes with the job. And any *fool* would have known it." She whirled away from him and out the bedroom door.

The phone was ringing. Travor didn't want to answer it. He was certain it was the beginning of many calls. How could he explain those pictures to his friends and neighbors? They'd think he was nuts.

It had been less than an hour since his scene with Erin, and his blood was gradually cooling to a simmer. She'd been right. He should have expected some publicity; he did expect it—just not so soon, not now, not yet. And especially not in his hometown.

Hell, not ever. If he was honest with himself, he wasn't sure he even wanted to participate in the Elvis videos. Had he ever really committed to it? He couldn't remember. The only thing he remembered was that one look into Erin's blue eyes, and he'd been willing to do anything. Even play the fool again.

Damn that telephone.

He yanked it up. "Yeah! Hello!"

"Uh-oh, I guess I'm too late. You've seen the layout."

"Lou?" He sat up straighter.

"I hope Erin's not nearby. I bet she's boilin'. But I had to strike while the iron was hot, Travor. People 'round here are still excited about you, and with Elvis Week coming up—"

He could feel his stomach burning. "Then it was you. Erin didn't have anything to do with it."

Lou guffawed into the phone. "You know better than that. I had to pay that photographer a fortune to tail you two. And that reminds me. If you see someone snooping around your neighborhood, don't shoot him, he's—"

Her voice became a whir in his ear. God, what had he done? He'd blasted Erin, saying all kinds of terrible things. He'd even accused her of prostituting herself to save the studio. Oh, God—

"Lou," he interrupted. "Lou, I can't talk right now. I'll get back to you."

"But Travor, wait! Tell Erin that—"

He hung up on her. He had things of his own to tell Erin.

Chapter Nine

Erin stepped out of the six-passenger single-engine plane that had brought her from Gilmer, Texas, to Memphis. A clean getaway, she thought, wondering if Travor even knew she was gone. He'd been so angry, she doubted he'd even tried to find her.

After walking out on him, Erin had thrown on some clothes and grabbed her purse with the intention of driving around until she'd cooled off, but as soon as she'd stepped out the door, Nellie had driven up. "You're in a huff," the woman had accused. "Guess you finally got around to confessin' your sins."

The moment the words were out of Nellie's mouth, Erin knew she had to get out of Rattan, Texas, immediately. She was tired of small-town living, small-town thinking and especially, small-town Elvises. And she told Nellie so.

Surprisingly, Nellie had laughed, hustled Erin into her little car and spirited her away. After a talk, Nellie had suggested they call a cousin who had a friend who had a son who owned a small plane, so Erin had negotiated a private flight to Memphis. It had cost her an arm and a leg. *And now here I am, riding in a taxi when I should be calling Lou to come and get me.* But she didn't want to call Lou. She didn't want to answer any questions about Travor Steele.

She could have driven all the way to Memphis, and probably should have, considering the amount of money she'd already spent, but in the back of her mind, she knew she needed to leave the van for Travor. If there was one thing she'd learned from Lou, it was not to burn bridges, no matter how angry you were. Erin knew Travor could ship the books and tapes to them, but he'd have to return to Memphis to get his motorcycle. Leaving the van for his convenience was the "Lou" thing to do. But aside from that, common sense had told her to get home as quickly as possible. If Lou had hired a photographer to follow them around snapping pictures, no telling what else was in the works. Whatever it was, Erin had to stop it before it happened. Especially under the circumstances.

Now that her feet were on familiar ground, rage was building—along with pain and regret and confusion.

Dear Lord, how did things get so out of control? she wondered. Sadistically, she replayed everything that had happened and Travor's accusations. All she wanted to do was cry.

It felt strange being back. Memphis seemed almost foreign to her. There weren't any country sounds or country smells.

And worse, there's no Travor Steele, she thought. Again she tried to force his memory from her mind, but she couldn't let go of him because even though she was mad as hell, she already missed him desperately. Funny how she had become so used to him, as if he were a part of her. As if they'd been together always.

It would have been nice to spend the rest of her life in Rattan, Texas, living with Travor day in and day out. Being a wife. Would I have been a good wife for him? she wondered. Or would I become bored with small-town living? And what about Max? Is he too much like his grandma to relax and smell the flowers? Erin suspected he was. But then it really didn't matter now. She looked out the window of the taxi at the familiar streets of Memphis.

Max would be in school; she hoped Lou was at the studio. All she wanted to do was stand in a steaming shower and shed tears for what could have been. Then again, why waste the energy? She wasn't cut out to be Mrs. Travor Steele any more than Lou was cut out to be a preacher's wife. Their lives were just too different from the norm. She blinked her eyes, trying to get rid of that prickly, teary feeling.

She saw the traffic jam as soon as the taxi turned onto their street. "I don't think I'm going to be able to get down there, lady."

"That's okay. I'll get out here and walk."

She got out of the cab and paid the driver, then made her way down the sidewalk. She saw scads of people crossing her street, and many more milling around Lou's front yard.

"Oh, God, what's going on?" Hopefully there wasn't another Elvis look-alike on the loose. She crossed Mrs. Tillotson's driveway and pushed her way across Lou's circular drive. The crowd parted, revealing Max and Lou standing on each side of Erin's queen-size bed. They stared at Erin. She stared back, shaking her head at what she was seeing. In bright red marker, on white poster board, she read: Jerry Lee Lewis Slept Here—$50. She burst into uncontrollable giggles.

"Jerry Lee Lewis...slept in my bed? I didn't know that." She could hardly talk for laughing so hard. "When did Jerry Lee Lewis sleep in my bed, Lou? When did Jerry Lee Lewis ever come to our house?" She doubled over, holding her stomach and trying desperately to control her laughter. Max and Lou looked at each other, totally confused.

"Mom! What's wrong?" Max yelled.

"Jerry Lee Lewis is wrong. Why not Waylon Jennings, Lou? Better yet, someone I could go for, like...like...Alan Jackson or Garth Brooks. Hey, how about Tim McGraw, Lou?"

She could feel the crowd of shoppers moving away from her as if they thought she was losing her mind. Was she? She couldn't quit laughing and she sure wasn't making any sense.

"Mom, it's just a sales pitch."

"No, it's not," Lou corrected, then turned her attention to Erin. "You said you wanted to get rid of this old frame. What's wrong with you? Are you okay?"

"Yeah, I'm okay. Everything is perfect...just peachy keen. My kid is skipping school, my mom is selling my bed and...and...and Travor is back in Texas—ma-ma-ma-ad as hell." She burst into tears. Loud, uncontrollable tears.

"I didn't have any tests today, Mom. Are you upset 'cause I'm cutting school?"

She sobbed louder.

"Mom?"

Lou put her arm around Max's shoulders. "She's not upset with you, baby."

Erin looked at them both, then raced past them, not caring one whit what the garage-sale shoppers thought of her. She reached the front door when she heard Lou exclaim.

"Max, your mama's finally fallen in love! And I've gone and screwed up royally."

Erin watched from her bedroom window as Lou hammered the For Sale sign in the ground in front of the house. Yesterday, after Erin had told Lou that Travor was out of the picture, Lou had sold her little convertible. Sure, it burned oil and had transmission problems, but Lou loved that little car because it had once belonged to Conway Twitty.

Everything was all mixed up. Nothing seemed right. And Erin felt like it was all her fault. If she'd moved in with Lou a year or two back, maybe this wouldn't be happening, but no, she'd insisted on her freedom. If she had worked on that supermarket promo instead of investing so much time in Travor Steele... Then again, if she'd stayed in Rattan, fought it out with Travor, pacified him in some way...

She felt the emptiness pressing against her insides. The pain was almost unbearable. She loved a man who hated her, and her entire family was suffering because of it. What could she do? There had to be something, or they would lose everything they had. But they could start over again, couldn't they? Isn't that what Lou always said? That because of every ending there was a new beginning? Hadn't Lou preached that all Erin's life? When Kyle was killed in the bus wreck, Lou had been there talking about new beginnings. And Max had been Erin's new beginning. When Elvis died, Lou had

had her own new beginning—this house. And Star Music Studio.

Lou's not depressed over this. Lou can start over with a smile on her face. For a moment, Erin loved her mother more than she'd ever loved her. She looked around her bedroom. No one had bought the Jerry Lee Lewis headboard. It leaned against the wall in the garage. Erin's mattress rested on the floor. She shook her head.

If I inherited anything from Lou, why wasn't it her sense of adventure? Why wasn't it her courage, her hardheadedness, or her...backbone? Then Travor's words came back to her. "You're just like your mother." *He's right,* she thought, just a little surprised. *I am like Lou.*

Erin loved the music business just as much as Lou did. And in spite of her actions, Erin had been excited about training Travor because she'd actually believed in Lou's project even though she wouldn't admit it. *The story of my life,* she thought. *I've spent all my time working against her even though I've always believed in her. Instead of letting her make wild deals and wrong decisions, why haven't I helped her, worked with her? Instead, I've made things more difficult for us all.*

Jutting out her chin, Erin buttoned the last button on her sleeveless white cotton shirt, then ran a hand through her hair. "Things are going to be different from now on. Because I'm just like my mother—smart, innovative, creative and courageous." She made a face in the mirror and whispered, "I sure as heck better start acting like it . . . or we're going to lose everything." She grabbed her white tennis shoes and ran out her bedroom door.

Lou was leaning on the For Sale sign, looking out at the neighborhood.

"Excuse me," Erin said and yanked the sign out of the ground. "You're counting your chickens again, Lou."

"We might as well make it look like going broke is our idea," Lou quipped. "If Travor's a no-show, then it's all downhill."

"Hey, what do you take me for? I left him our van and all the books and tapes. He knows where we live." She winked at Lou. "Besides that, he has to come back for his motorcycle. Then we'll grab him."

Lou grinned. "But what good will it do? You said he's so hung up on looking foolish, that we could never pull it off using him to portray a nineties Elvis. I think you'd better poke that sign right back down in the ground."

Erin put an arm around her mother's shoulders. "Let's go have a cup of chocolate raspberry coffee and talk this over. I'm going to explain to you just why we don't need Travor Steele from Rattan, Texas. And it has to do with teamwork."

Lou frowned. "Teamwork? We've always been a team, so what's that got to do with it?"

Erin squeezed her mother's shoulder and fought the lump in her throat. "So tell me, *Mom,* do we have anyone entered in those look-alike contests next week? And have you got any of those delicious New Orleans pralines left?"

Travor stood in the mud looking up at the derrick. It was impressive, sort of majestic and, he imagined, almost as grand as the Statue of Liberty. It fell into the same category, in Travor's mind, as apple pie, football and Texas longhorns. Sort of all-American.

Ever since Erin had left, three days ago, Travor had spent his time at the well site. His house was filled with her scent, her memory; he hated being there alone, without her. The small cramped trailer on-site was the only place he could be free of her. Who was he trying to kid? He'd never be free of her. Little things she'd said, her musical laughter haunted him day and night. God, why couldn't he banish her from his mind?

Because he'd never known a woman like her. He'd shared things with her that he'd never shared with anyone. Like how he'd felt when his mother died; the fear, the loneliness, the decisions he'd had to make. And about his very first investment experience. How second-guessing himself had almost scared him senseless and that he'd almost pulled out of the oil venture because of his own doubts. He remembered the look on her face as she'd listened to him, wide-eyed and with real interest. When he'd told her that he'd spent every free moment at the well site, almost driving the crew crazy with his many questions, she'd grinned knowingly, but she'd laughed aloud when he'd admitted that he'd even slept on location at times, afraid he'd miss something if he went home. The memory of her voice sent goose bumps up his spine.

Travor remembered that first investment as a heady experience, how it had changed his life. He realized now that he could compare it with meeting Erin. She was a heady experience, too. And God knew, she'd certainly changed his life.

After Lou had called about the publicity stunt, Travor had rushed into Erin's room with every intention of apologizing, begging her forgiveness. He would have groveled, done whatever it took to get her to forget everything he'd said. But she wasn't there. She'd walked out on him, disappeared as if he wasn't worth spit. And then later that evening, Nellie had appeared, explaining Erin's departure. He closed his eyes, trying to do away with the memory.

It really didn't matter much that she wasn't involved in the newspaper promo. What mattered was that she'd deserted him, left him alone to face the music.

And there had been music. Every day the tabloids came out with pictures of Elvis, Travor and Erin. While it stunned him to see his face staring back at him from the newsstands, it just felt silly now—not at all like the first time.

God, that had been a shock, seeing Elvis so heavy, so completely different from the sexy, virile young man Travor had been emulating. And that's what really disturbed him. That horrible picture. It had almost knocked the breath out of him. It was as if they'd traded places.

But none of that mattered now. Because he'd decided the deal was off. He couldn't be Elvis. He didn't want to be Elvis. And he didn't want to have anything more to do with Erin Weller. If she'd cared anything about him at all, she would have stayed and fought it out. Wouldn't she? Wasn't that what people in love did? Fought it out, fought for love, fought to make things right again. He ran a hand through his thick black hair, and shook his head.

Hell, he didn't know what people in love did. He'd never been in love. All he knew was that no matter how badly he'd hurt when Celeste had deserted him, this was a hundred times worse...and he sure as hell didn't know why.

"I'm glad this head-scratchin' time is over, Travor." The old tool-pusher who had walked up beside him grinned and took a red rag out of his pocket to wipe his hands. During another time, another investment, Sam had talked Travor into drilling a couple of hundred feet more, and on Sam's gut feeling, Travor had approached the investors. Thank God, Sam had been right; otherwise, they all would have lost a hell of a lot of money. And Sam was the only person he knew who hadn't commented on the Elvis crap.

"You're a good man, Sam."

"Yeah, well, I think I'll go on home and tell the old lady that. She ain't been too happy with me lately."

Travor chuckled, and looked back up at the tall derrick. He expected Sam to walk away from him and when he didn't, Travor looked back, curiously. "Is there something else, Sam?"

The old man turned a deep red. "Well, Travor, I reckon this is pretty dumb, but Martha Jean...she was wondering..." He fumbled around, ran a hand through his thinning hair. He cleared his throat and began again. "We got all them tabloids that your pictures showed up in. Martha Jean would be real obliged if you'd drop by the house someday, autograph them for her."

Travor couldn't hide his surprise. Sam shook his head. "You'll learn, Travor, that when it comes to women, the head-scratchin' time never ends. A man just has to learn to live with it. And my friend, you can take that little tip as gospel."

Travor was still musing over Sam's advice when he got to his house. It was time to face the emptiness, the loneliness, no matter how badly it hurt. He was surprised to see Nellie sweeping his front porch.

When he got out of the van, Nellie shook her head. "I wondered when you was coming back here. You been living at that well, ain't you? I figured as much, so I been coming to feed the dogs."

He walked toward her, knowing he should thank her for her concern, but resenting her presence, her interference. He'd wanted to be able to walk into his house and inhale the intoxicating scent he missed, he longed for. Now he'd have to watch himself because Nellie noticed everything.

"You hungry? I got one of my veggie pies in the oven."

"Sounds good," he answered, walking past her.

The house reeked of pine scent like it always did when Nellie cleaned. Travor held his breath, gritted his teeth. She'd wiped away every trace of Erin with just a swoop of the dustcloth. He resented it, but at the same time, he was grateful for it. He had enough reminders: like the sweet, clean scent of her white-gold hair, and the feel of her arms around him, the warmth and softness of her skin.

Damn, how the hell was he ever going to get Erin Weller out of his mind?

"Sit yourself down and I'll shovel it up for you. 'Oprah' starts in half an hour and if you don't mind, I'd like to hang around and watch it. It's a lot more fun watching her on the big screen. Today they got some women on there who were married to Elvis impersonators. They're gonna tell what it was like being hung up on men who were hung up on imitating a legend."

"Oh, for Pete's sake!" Travor grumbled, washing his hands at the kitchen sink. "Has the entire world gone Elvis crazy?"

Nellie shrugged. "This has been going on for a good while. Seems we just never paid much mind to it around here. And from all those articles I've been reading, Elvis is as big a star now as he ever was. I done joined three fan clubs."

"Nellie!" Stunned, he sat down at the table.

But Nellie continued, moving about the kitchen as if it was hers. "Several of us been thinking about starting our own fan club. I hadn't seen none around here, and one of them articles says he came through East Texas a bunch. Played over in Gladewater a lot. Well, with you looking like you do, and able to impersonate him, it only seems right that—"

"Have you lost your mind?" Travor looked at her incredulously. "You can't believe I'd do such a thing. I'd be the laughingstock of Texas. It'd be worse than when Celeste left me standing at the altar. Oh, no. It may take me a while, but I eventually catch on."

Nellie put her hands on her hips. "Now what are you talking about, Travor Lee? Catch on to what?"

Travor grunted and got up from the table. He hadn't discussed Celeste with anyone other than Erin since the day she'd disappeared. And now that he thought about it, no one had discussed her with him. He ran a hand through his hair and began to pace. "I know I was the laughingstock when Celeste didn't show up. I'll never forget it as long as I live. You were sitting in the second row. Mrs. Lucas was at the piano. MaeBelle Shirley was standing there singing and we were all waiting. When MaeBelle had sung 'Oh Promise Me' for the third time, I saw you wink at Mrs. Lucas who looked over at MaeBelle and winked and—" He rubbed a hand across his face. "You all expected it, didn't you? You all knew Celeste wasn't going to show up."

Nellie sat herself down at the long pine table. "Lord, Lord, Lord, Lord, Lord," she mumbled. "Is that what you thought? That we all knew something you didn't know? Is that why you ain't been hanging around your own hometown 'cause you're frettin' over something like that?"

"I felt like a fool. How else should I feel?" he demanded.

Nellie got up from the table. "Travor Lee, we never thought you'd be so hurt. If we'd known—"

Travor frowned. "What do you mean, 'If we'd known'?"

Nellie smiled.

"Did ya'll have something to do with Celeste leaving me, Nellie?"

She shrugged. "If you remember, not too many of us liked Celeste Fillmore."

"Yeah, I remember, but—"

"We didn't think she was the type of girl your mother would have enjoyed having as a daughter-in-law, so..."

"So what?" Travor asked, suspiciously when Nellie paused.

"So...we had a special prayer chain going. All us women in the Scripture Club. And we all prayed that the Lord would intervene on your behalf and you wouldn't marry Celeste Fillmore."

Travor looked at her, his mouth hanging open. He couldn't believe what he was hearing.

"So when I winked at old lady Lucas, and she winked at MaeBelle, we were just confirming the power of the Lord to answer prayer. We just prayed you'd be delivered from the clutches of Celeste, and you was. The whole town knew it and nobody thought you was a fool—except you, I guess."

Travor was still gaping, mouth open. Could Nellie be telling the truth? It had all been in his mind?

Nellie continued, not paying any attention to Travor's state of shock. "Why, Celeste not showing up was the biggest miracle any of us had ever witnessed. Reverend Perkins agrees," Nellie confided.

Travor moved around the kitchen, shaking his head. It had never happened the way he'd imagined. No one had thought a thing about Celeste not showing up at their wedding because—he grinned broadly—they'd planned it that way.

Oh, he was a fool, all right, but he'd done it to himself. And only because he was scared to take a chance, risk his heart, fall in love. Why, any fool could see Erin was different. She was worth taking any risk for. Suddenly he laughed. He felt free and young and unburdened. He grabbed Nellie and tried to swing her around but she fought him off.

"Quit acting silly, boy!" she demanded.

"I can't," he answered, grinning from ear to ear. "Nellie, dish me up a huge plate of that veggie pie of yours, then you get on the horn and call your prayer group. I need some more help."

"With that Memphis girl?" Nellie asked.

He quirked an eyebrow at her. "Nellie, don't you go messing things up for me. I love her."

Nellie grinned from ear to ear. "And whether she knows it or not, she loves you."

The living room was strewn with balls of paper. Travor sat on the sofa with the remote control pointed at the television. He clicked a pen against his knee. In this movie, Elvis was sitting on some monkey bars singing the "confidence song" to a bunch of kids. Travor jotted notes on a sheet of paper, then rewound the scene to watch it again.

Analyzing the movies and songs, Travor felt as if he could slot Elvis right up there with apple pie, football and Texas longhorns. This guy was all-American all the way. But there was something more—something Travor couldn't quite put his finger on. He looked at the paper around him. He had categorized the musical scenes: beaches, nightclubs, singing to women, singing to kids, singing to animals, party scenes. For some reason, he was beginning to feel a little like Lou. Fanatical.

"So how would one market Elvis in the nineties?" Travor wondered aloud, shuffling the papers. If he could find the answer to that question, he might be able to solve Erin and Lou's financial problems.

He sat back on the sofa and thought about all the movies he'd watched. What did they have in common? Music. Girls. Fast cars or motorcycles. Love. Kids. Money or the lack thereof. He rubbed his chin and squinted his eyes as an idea began to take shape, and he jotted notes as quickly as he could.

Two hours later, he picked up the Kimbie Love demo tape. "Now, what should we do with you?"

Chapter Ten

Erin tossed her purse on the sofa as soon as she entered the house. "That was a pitiful contest. I've never seen so many papier-mâché and plastic belts in all my life. And those costumes..."

Lou followed her daughter inside the room and slammed herself into the bucket chair. "If those dudes are going to imitate Elvis, they should take the trouble to do it right. After all, just how much can an extra-wide diamond-encrusted genuine leather belt set you back?"

Erin laughed. "When that eighty-year-old Elvis whipped off his cape and got tangled up in it, then fell off the stage, I couldn't believe it. Thank goodness, there were paramedics standing by." She laughed again, slipping off her shoes, then stretching out on the sofa. "I hate to admit it, Lou, but if Travor had been here he would've won, hands down."

Lou sat up straight in her chair. "I'm glad to hear you say that. Why don't we call him—just to see how he's doing?"

"No."

"But I want my tapes and books back. It's been almost three weeks."

"Not quite two," Erin corrected.

"Seems longer."

Erin smiled. "That's because you are a very impatient lady." But she agreed with her mother. It did seem longer. And she was beginning to wonder if she'd ever see Travor Steele again. In the middle of the night she was certain she heard him calling her name. It would wake her, and then her imagination would really get wild: the scent of his after-shave would drift through the room; the sound of his laughter would tease her memory, seemingly vibrating from within her bedroom walls. For no good reason, her hands would tingle as if palming his thick, coarse chest hair. She never knew if she was dreaming or his memory was actually haunting her.

Rubbing her hands on her denim jeans, Erin shook her head, trying her best to clear it. If she didn't know better, she'd think someone had put a spell on her. But it was no spell. She knew exactly why she couldn't sleep or eat or focus on work. Because she loved him. And it was going to take everything she had within her to live without him. *But I can do it, and I will do it,* she vowed. With Lou and Max's help. Thank God, they weren't interfering like they usually did.

Erin had sat them down and given them some straight talk about Travor Steele. She told them he was too afraid of looking foolish to get involved in their Elvis project. She tried to make them understand how different his life had been from theirs, and that because of it, he couldn't be free, couldn't let himself live the way they lived. "Look at us," she'd told them. "We make fools of ourselves every day of the week. He couldn't handle that."

Lou took exception to the phrase "every day of the week." Max was concerned about getting their van back, but they both agreed with Erin and promised to leave Travor Steele alone, not interfere. She didn't admit to them that she loved him, that she missed him terribly, that she could hardly stand the thought of living her life without him.

Suddenly the phone rang, and Erin jumped at the intrusive sound.

"Are you going to get it this time?" Lou asked.

"No. I told you I don't want to talk with him. But you can if you like—as long as you don't try to talk him into the Elvis thing again."

Lou shook her head. "I'd better not. I don't trust myself. I'd be begging him to come back to Memphis."

They both stared at the phone before Erin ran to the front door and yelled for Max, who was outside talking with some neighbor kids. "Hurry, you have to answer it—just in case."

"Oh, Mom... What do you guys do when I'm not home?"

"We forward it to the office. Now, hurry!"

She watched as Max picked up the phone. "Hello... Yeah... Yeah... Sure. I think so... No... Okay." Then he placed it back in its cradle and raced for the door.

"Hey, you. Who was that?" Erin yelled.

Max turned to look at her. "You mean you want to know?"

She put her hands on her hips. "Don't get smart. Was that who I think it was?"

"Who do you think it was?" Max asked.

"Max Weller, you tell me if that was Travor Steele right this minute or your weekend is canceled as of tomorrow, immediately after school."

"I have tutoring after school tomorrow."

Erin squinted one eye in warning, then watched as Max opened the door and stuck his head out. "Hey, guys, I'm grounded. See you next week."

Stunned, Erin stared at her son, not knowing what to think. She didn't see him shoot Lou a thumbs-up sign as he raced past her to his bedroom.

Travor pulled the Stetson down over his brow as he braked for the red light. He'd just reached Memphis and he had fifteen minutes to get to the school to pick up Max. He didn't want to be late. Travor had to find out what the hell was going on, and the kid was the only one who seemed to be talking to him. If you could call his monosyllabic telephone dialogue actually talking. Not much different than the one conversation he'd had with Erin, he thought. He'd apologized profusely for the way he'd acted toward her, the terrible things he'd said, and she'd accepted his apology but she'd been cool, cryptic. And after that, she'd never answered the phone again. Come to think of it, neither had Lou.

Travor rubbed his chin. Had they lost interest in the Elvis videos? He thought it was odd that Lou wasn't sending him messages to get back to Memphis. Or that she hadn't requested her books and videos returned immediately, if not sooner.

But none of that mattered now because he had one heck of a proposition for them. One that would not only save Star Music Studio, but put it in the big time. He'd worked day and night for a week on the proposal, watching the Elvis movies, the documentaries, and skimming the books just to be able to talk intelligently about Elvis Presley. He had tried to view his idea from Lou's point of view, yet ask himself every question that Erin might ask. He knew Erin would challenge the proposal, point out all the risks involved, but he was ready for her. He'd taken the same approach he took when introducing a new venture to his investors. He'd brazenly pointed out the possible losses as well as the potential profits. And that's what he would do with Lou and Erin.

If Lou Weller sincerely wanted to keep Elvis's memory alive, then this was the route to go, the only way to promote Elvis in the nineties. And the only way to make money doing it. He looked over at the briefcase in the passenger seat. Travor had listed the specific movies, scenes and songs, and had written down suggestions for exactly what could be done with them. The trick would be in convincing Lou that the world didn't need any more Elvis impersonators. It's a damn good idea, he thought, gripping the steering wheel tightly. It'll work. I know it'll work. In fact, he was so impressed with the possibilities of success, that he was willing to finance the venture. He wondered how Erin would feel about that?

He grinned and tugged at the Stetson again, picturing Erin's face in his mind. "And lady, do I have a deal for you."

Travor saw Max waiting beneath a tree in front of the school. His bike rested against his leg. Travor tooted the horn and laughed as Max waved wildly. He pulled to a stop beside the boy.

Max slid the van door open and heaved his bike inside. "Hi, I told Mom I'd be staying late today because of some tutoring. Are you here for good, now? Mom said you have lots of dogs. What's that in your hair? You don't look too much like Elvis anymore."

Travor laughed and reached out to pull the bike farther into the van. He removed his hat so Max could get a better look. "What do you think? A friend of mine back home gave me some gray stuff to comb through it. Can't take any chances around here."

"That's awesome. I use that stuff at Halloween sometimes." Max climbed into the front seat. "Elvis week is over but we still got lots of tourists around. Grandma said everyone thinks they can be an Elvis impersonator. You should have seen some of those contests. You woulda won hands down. They even had a woman. Can you believe that? A woman Elvis impersonator! You woulda won hands down! Mom even said so."

"So, how is your mom?" Travor asked. "Why won't she talk to me on the phone?"

Max grinned broadly; mischievously, Travor thought, but he couldn't be sure.

"Mom's in love," the boy answered.

Travor jerked his head around toward Max. "What do you mean, your mom is in love? With who?"

Max shrugged and looked out the window. "Don't ask me. That's just what Grandma told me. Didn't make any sense to me, either."

Max's words terrified Travor. Was it true? Had Erin fallen in love with someone else? Had his stupidity pushed her into the arms of another man? For the first time, Travor looked at his life without Erin. All he could see was a lone motorcycle rider cruising down a deserted road. That's not how he wanted it to be. He didn't like what he saw. He wanted Erin with him, pressed solidly against his back. He wanted to feel her arms around his waist and the insides of her thighs squeezing tightly against his. And he wanted Max with him, too. What was the point of going places, seeing things, if the people he loved weren't with him?

"Your mother can't be in love with anyone else," he said, shooting a desperate glance toward Max.

Max jutted out his chin just the way Erin always did. "What's it to you? You're not gonna stay, anyway. You told us you were gonna travel all around the country and see things."

Travor gripped the steering wheel tightly. It was the first time he'd seen the insecure, vulnerable side of Max. He didn't like it. He didn't like knowing he could hurt this kid and his mother. "Things have changed," he whispered, fighting a lump in his throat.

"How?"

Suddenly, all he wanted to do was see that freckle-faced grin. "You ever seen a buddy seat? One of those little sidecars that go on a motorcycle?"

Max shook his head.

"I haven't, either, but we're gonna check 'em out."

Max looked out the window of the van so Travor wouldn't see his grin. His grandma said the plan would work. Now it was time for the next step.

"Mom's gotten real weird. She tried on one of Grandma's eye patches and said she might start wearing one, too."

Travor frowned. "Why? No offense, Max, but isn't one nut in the family enough?"

Max shrugged. "She said she's just like Grandma. I never thought so. Grandma was always a lot more fun."

Laughing, Travor pounded the steering wheel, realizing what Max had said. Erin had been quoting him. He'd told her she was a lot like Lou—and now she was accepting it. That's a good sign, he thought. He felt foolish and excited when a prickly feeling occurred just behind his eyelids. It was all Travor could do to keep from grabbing the boy and hugging him. Instead, he reached over and ruffled Max's thick red hair. "Thanks, kid. I owe you."

They grinned at each other, then Max snapped his fingers. "Uh-oh, I forgot to tell you—Grandma's giving everything away."

"All her Elvis collection?" Travor questioned.

"Some of it. And her Jerry Lee Lewis stuff. She used to like him, too. And her Carl Perkins stuff. Her birthday is April 9th, the same day as his. She says they're birthday twins."

"Why?" Travor asked.

"Because they were born on the same day."

"No, I mean why is she getting rid of it all?"

"She donated it to a museum. She's talked about it for a long time and she said now was the time to do it. She told Mom that it was cumber-cumbersome or something, and that they had to be ready when opportunity strikes."

Travor wheeled the van into a fast-food joint, killed the engine and turned to Max. "I'll treat you to some ice cream, Max, old buddy, while you tell me everything. Then I've got to get you home. Opportunity is fixin' to strike."

Max popped the seat belt, grinning from ear to ear. He knew opportunity was fixing to strike, because he'd played Cupid—just the way his grandma had told him to.

* * *

Travor hid his disappointment when Lou pulled open the door. The kid had told him his mom might still be at the studio. That was okay. He'd run things by Lou first. Erin would probably be a harder sell, but Lou—he knew how Elvis-hungry she was.

Lou looked him up and down. "What's with the gray hair? Looks like you can be anybody you want to be. Or did Erin do that to you?" She laughed at her own joke and Max joined in.

Travor moved past her into the room. "Why haven't you been answering the phone, accepting my calls?"

"We made a deal with Erin. Told her we'd stay completely out of everything. And we have, haven't we, Max?"

Max grinned. "Well-l-l, sorta."

Travor shook his head. "This was one time you probably shouldn't have." He held his briefcase up. "Are you still interested in working with me?" he asked.

Lou looked surprised. "Well, yeah, but you aren't going to fly off into the sunset once we get rolling, are you? 'Cause once we get started—"

"Lady," Travor interrupted, "we're going all the way with this one."

Lou lifted her glittery orange eye patch and grinned. "All the way where?"

"Let's go into the office and discuss it," Travor said, walking toward the kitchen. "And Max, if your mom comes in, keep her occupied until we're finished. I've got a separate deal for her."

* * *

Erin paced the floor. She'd peeled the polish off two fingernails, gnawed the inside of her lip until it was raw and now she was popping her knuckles.

"Mom, we learned in health that popping your knuckles causes damage to your cartilages."

"Why won't you tell me what's going on? You obviously know something. What did Travor tell you? What kind of deal was he talking about?" She sat down on the sofa with her son and grabbed a pillow to fiddle with. "Tell me exactly what he said about me." But she couldn't sit still. Jumping up, she squeezed the throw pillow and paced the floor once again. "No, don't tell me. I really don't want to know." She looked at Max expectantly. When it was obvious he wasn't going to respond, she stopped. "Okay, okay, give it to me straight. Did he say anything about me?"

Max giggled, obviously enjoying the moment. "He said, did she say anything about me?" Erin tossed the pillow at his freckled face.

"Mom, you sound just like the girls at school." He made his voice high and feminine. "Did he say anything about me? Do you think he likes me? Oh, he's just so-o-o cute." Max laughed and rolled around on the sofa.

"Max, this is a little more serious than that."

"Why?" he asked.

"Because—well, it's... it's different."

"Grandma said you're in love."

"Oh, no, you didn't tell him that, did you?"

Max didn't answer and Erin flopped back down on the sofa. "Max, you did, didn't you? You told him I'm in love with him."

"Heck, no, I didn't tell him you were in love with him. I just told him you're in love."

Erin groaned and rubbed her forehead with her hand. "What did he say?"

Max laughed. "He said, 'Who with?'"

Erin snorted in a disgusted manner. "As if he didn't know."

"Gee, Mom, are you really in love with Travor? I hope so, 'cause he's great. Travor's radical. I think Travor's—"

"Max, please. Did you tell him anything else that I need to know?"

"Well-l-l." Max rubbed his chin and pretended to think.

Erin glared at him. "Why am I putting myself through this? I don't have to wait out here. This is my house, too!" She moved toward the hallway that led to the kitchen. "I don't care what he said. I'm going right in there and—"

Travor appeared, and leaned against the doorjamb. "And what?"

Erin felt her face steam. God, he looked handsome even with that weird gray hair. His black jeans hugged his muscular thighs. Erin had never seen him in a Western jacket. He looked every inch the country gentleman. Getting a grip on her emotions, she jutted out her chin. "And . . . find out what's going on."

Travor wiggled his finger at her, motioning her toward the kitchen. "You're just in time."

They sat at the kitchen table. Travor's heart was pounding double time, but not because of the deal he was going to present them. It was Erin. She looked so damned glad to see him. Even though she had jutted out her chin in that obstinate way, her eyes twinkled and that little grin played around her lips. It was all he could do to keep from planting a big wet kiss right on the end of her pert little nose. Time for that later. Once he got her alone, he wanted a real kiss, and he didn't plan on letting her up for air.

"He's done nothing but tease me, Erin. And talk about going partners. I got a partner. Two of them, if you count Max."

"Are you saying you don't want me as a partner?"

Lou pulled the eye patch back down over her eye and rubbed her chin. She looked at Erin and Erin looked back. Travor could feel the mental conversation going on between them.

"Come on, ladies. You know I'm honest. And your plan worked. You knew it would."

"What plan?" Erin asked.

Travor grunted. "The Elvis plan. How can anyone eat, drink and live Elvis Presley and not get hooked somehow? Isn't that what you were counting on? Me getting hooked?"

Erin and Lou looked at each other and shrugged as if they had no idea what he was talking about.

Travor laughed and shook his head. Maybe they hadn't planned on him getting hooked. Maybe it had just accidentally happened that way.

"So you're telling us you got a good idea. So good that you want a piece of the action." Lou patted the table with both palms. "Don't keep us in suspense. Get on with it."

Travor leaned forward and took a deep breath. This was more exciting than the oil business. "Ladies," he said, eyeing Lou and then Erin. Then he paused. "This is so good, I'm shocked that no one's done it. Someone will—it's just a matter of time."

Erin could feel the hair standing on the back of her neck. He was serious. "What is it, Travor?" she asked, her voice a mere whisper.

He looked at her. "Kids," he replied. "Kids and Elvis."

Lou frowned, but Travor saw the idea click in Erin's mind. He continued, concentrating on helping Lou see the big picture. "Tell me, Lou, why do you want to do this? Is it just for the money?"

Lou was indignant. "Hell, no! I want to show the world that Elvis isn't dead. He's very much alive—in his music, his movies and—"

"Right! Great. That's exactly what we can do. But you don't do that with people who already know the man. They've made up their minds about liking him. They either do or they don't. But the kids, Lou—the little kids—now, there's our market."

"Then just why hasn't somebody already done it?"

Erin answered for him. "Because everyone else is busy with cartoon characters and purple dinosaurs and—"

Travor nodded, too excited to let her finish. "In almost every Elvis movie, there are scenes with kids. I swear the guy was a natural. He sings 'Old MacDonald' on the back of a truck. He sings to a hound dog in one of them. He climbs on monkey bars, and he plays around with two little Asian girls—and there's that carousel scene, remember?"

Erin joined in. "We can make videos for kids using cuts from the movies—or maybe even—"

Lou jumped up from the table. "Move over, purple dinosaur, here comes Elvis. Watch out Big Bird, you got competition! When do we start?"

Travor stood with her. "I've already got people working on it. As soon as I give them the word, they'll fly into Memphis and meet with you. Of course, you know we're going to have to contact representatives from his estate to set up—"

"I know, I know. I've done it before. That's no problem." She looked at Erin, then back at Travor. "Partners, huh? Why don't you just float me a loan?"

"I've done my homework, Lou. A good video can cost anywhere from fifty thousand to a hundred thousand dollars, depending on the location, equipment, size of cast and the time it takes to make it. Are you saying you'd rather have a onetime loan than a wealthy partner?"

Lou lifted herself to sit on the kitchen counter and stared at Erin. Once again, Travor could feel the mental conversation between them. Erin moved next to him. "What Lou is saying is . . . if you just give her a loan, then you can hop on your bike and take off across country. No more problems with the Weller family."

Travor ran a hand through his hair. "You people are sure trying to get me on my bike and out of here."

"Isn't that what you want?" Erin asked.

"No, it's not what I want. I want a few weekend jaunts with a wife and a son." He reached for her and pulled her into his arms. "Erin, I realize now I was running away. I thought everyone back home was laughing at me behind my back. I was wrong." He nuzzled the top of her white-gold hair. "I want you, Erin. I love you. And I want to be a part of your crazy life, even if it means wearing jumpsuits and lip-syncing 'Hound Dog' for the rest of my life. Will you marry me?"

She pulled away from him, and looked deep into his eyes. "Oh, Travor, I love you—"

Before she could finish, the kitchen door burst open. "I already said yes, Mom. I'm gonna have a buddy seat on the Harley, a tree house out in the woods and all the dogs I want."

Lou joined in. "And I'm gonna have a *silent* partner." When Erin and Travor looked at her, she quickly explained. "I think you'll be a better husband, father and son-in-law if you don't have to wear leather jumpsuits for the rest of your life." She pushed the eye patch to the top of her head. "Don't you?"

Travor hugged Erin to him, laughing. "I totally agree."

Chapter Eleven

Erin stood in the middle of the room, twirling around in her ivory wedding dress. It was the second time she'd worn it.

"Hurry up, Travor, we're going to be late."

"I would never be late for my own wedding," he answered, fiddling with his tie. "Especially my *second* wedding."

Erin laughed. "I'll bet people think we're crazy having two ceremonies—especially big ones—within ten days of each other."

"We had to. One for Lou and her Memphis crowd and one for Nellie and the Scripture Club. Can you imagine what we'd go through if we'd denied either woman the pleasure of planning these shindigs?"

He moved toward her and took her in his arms. "Why don't we just stay here...skip right to the honeymoon?"

"Not a bad idea," she whispered, loving the way she fit against him. They were perfect for each other, like connecting pieces of a puzzle.

"It's going to be tough topping that Memphis affair," he mused. "Lou outdid herself."

Erin nuzzled his neck. "Mmm, it's going to be tough topping that New Orleans honeymoon. You really *outdid* yourself."

He laughed and nuzzled back. "I did, didn't I? Where are you taking me on our next honeymoon?"

They'd divided everything. Lou and Nellie planned the weddings, Erin and Travor each planned a honeymoon.

"I can't tell you. It's a secret," she teased.

"Hey, no secrets—that was in our Memphis vows."

She took his face between her hands and kissed him. "No secrets. I'll let you know where I'm taking you after this Texas wedding—if we ever get to the church."

Just as the words left her mouth, the telephone rang. Travor looked at his watch. "Uh-oh, we really are late. I'll bet that's Nellie."

"Or Max."

"Or even Lou. Let's let it ring." He looked at her and feigned surprise. "Just look at us. We're beginning to take our weddings for granted."

Erin straightened his tie. "Oh, Travor, I hope this ceremony is every bit as perfect as the first one. Kimbie Love sang beautifully. You had a great idea when you suggested she channel that wild, sensual tone into a more traditional-type song. It works. But weren't you surprised that Lou would go for real wedding tunes like 'I Love You Truly'?"

"Lou wanted everything to be beautiful and perfect for her only child."

"It was, but I still expected something along the lines of the 'Hawaiian Wedding Song' with an Elvis impersonator singing it."

"Would you have objected to that?" Travor asked, slipping into his jacket.

"Of course not. If it wasn't for Elvis—"

The phone started again, interrupting her. "Let's get out of here," she said and they ran out the door without answering the phone.

Taking her hand, Travor started toward the van, but Erin stopped him. "Wait." She looked toward the Harley with its brand-new sidecar and grinned wickedly. "What do you think?"

"What about your hair?"

"I can fix it at the church. Let's go."

They raced toward the black-and-red motorcycle and Travor picked Erin up in his arms, placing her inside the buddy seat. "This is wild," he said.

"Not any wilder than your blue suede shoes," she answered, frowning down at his feet.

He tweaked her nose then straddled the bike, taking a moment to admire the funny blue suede shoes he'd found in New Orleans. Erin grinned and jabbed him in the thigh.

The weather was perfect—warm and sunny, a typical East Texas September day. When they reached the church, Erin smiled at the number of cars parked sporadically on the gravel lot.

She stood in the seat and ran both hands through her hair. "Looks like the whole town turned out."

"They were all invited. This time they expect to see some action."

Erin laughed. "I think that's why you insisted we get married in Memphis first, so you'd know I'd show up here."

He kissed her on the tip of her nose, then lifted her to the ground. "I knew I couldn't put anything over on you. Let's hurry. I want to get to that honeymoon."

Erin could feel herself blushing. Their first honeymoon was a long weekend at the French Quarter Inn. Erin couldn't have been more pleased. She loved Travor's sensitivity and his romanticism. New Orleans *had* meant something to him. As much as it had meant to her. On their first honeymoon, they'd lain in bed together and confessed exactly how they'd felt during their first trip to New Orleans, sitting in their separate rooms—alone. It was something they could laugh about now, but they promised to always communicate their feelings. It was even written into their wedding vows.

Erin was looking forward to surprising Travor with their second honeymoon—once again at the French Quarter Inn in New Orleans.

Turning toward the church, she could hear music, and then she saw Max push open the bright-red double doors. "Mom! Travor! You're late and everyone's here. Aunt Nellie is fit to be tied."

"*Aunt* Nellie?" Travor questioned with a quirk of his eyebrow.

Erin grinned. "She told him to call her Aunt Nellie. She said he was going to fit right in around here."

"Now what does that mean?" Travor asked.

"I shudder to think."

Inside the church, wall-to-wall people sat, waiting. The small building smelled of flowers, candles and various after-shaves and colognes. The piano and organ harmonized, playing something Erin didn't recognize.

As planned, she and Travor walked arm in arm down the aisle. Suddenly, the music changed to something Erin did recognize: the "Hawaiian Wedding Song." She looked up at Travor, who smiled knowingly.

"You knew, didn't you?" she whispered.

"They ran a few ideas by me."

"Now I understand why you insisted on buying those shoes. Should I be worried?" she asked.

"Only if you start messing around with my chest hair."

In seconds, they were standing in front of Reverend Perkins, repeating vows. And then Erin was surprised when the pastor asked if Max would join the couple. Her son left Lou's side and marched up between them, grinning from ear to ear.

"Max Weller, you're a lucky young man to be a part of this loving family. I understand you have something you'd like to say."

Max took a sheet of paper from his tuxedo pocket and unfolded it. Then he cleared his throat and looked solemnly up at Travor, never glancing at his notes.

"I've always had the best family in the world—my mom and my grandma. I never thought it could be any better. Then you came, Travor. And it was awesome. You made me miss not having a dad." He took a step closer to Travor. "But I've got one now—"

Erin watched as Travor put his arm around Max and pulled him close. Tears slid down her cheeks.

Then the music began and MaeBelle Shirley moved toward the pianist. She sang "Love Me Tender" with tears running down her own cheeks. Erin was certain the song had never sounded so beautiful. She reached for Travor's hand and squeezed; he smiled and squeezed back. Together, they looked down at Max just in time to see him give a thumbs-up to Lou, then wink at Nellie. Nellie grinned and winked at Mrs. Lucas and Mrs. Lucas passed it on to MaeBelle, who passed it on to Reverend Perkins who, in turn, winked at...

Erin looked up at Travor, a quizzical expression on her face. He shrugged. "That's just lovin' you, baby..." he explained in his best Elvis voice.

* * * * *

COMING NEXT MONTH

#1144 MOST WANTED DAD—Arlene James
Fabulous Fathers/This Side of Heaven
Amy Slater knew the teenage girl next door needed a sympathetic ear—as did her father, Evans Kincaid. But Amy found it hard to be just a *friend* to the sexy lawman, even though she'd sworn never to love again....

#1145 DO YOU TAKE THIS CHILD?—Marie Ferrarella
The Baby of the Month Club
One night of passion with handsome Slade Garret left Dr. Sheila Pollack expecting nothing...except a baby! When Slade returned and demanded marriage, Sheila tried to resist. But Slade caught her at a weak moment—while she was in labor!

#1146 REILLY'S BRIDE—Patricia Thayer
Women were in demand in Lost Hope, Wyoming, so why did Jenny Murdock want stubborn rancher Luke Reilly, the only man *not* looking for a wife? Now Jenny had to convince Reilly he needed a bride....

#1147 MOM IN THE MAKING—Carla Cassidy
The Baker Brood
Bonnie Baker was in Casey's Corners to hide from love, not to be swept away by town catch Russ Blackburn! Gorgeous, devilish Russ got under her skin all right...but could Bonnie ever risk love again?

#1148 HER VERY OWN HUSBAND—Lauryn Chandler
Rose Honeycutt had just blown out her birthday candles when a handsome drifter showed up on her doorstep. Cowboy Skye Hanks was everything she'd wished for, but would his mysterious past keep them from a future together?

#1149 WRANGLER'S WEDDING—Robin Nicholas
Rachel Callahan would do anything to keep custody of her daughter. So when Shane Purcell proposed a pretend engagement, Rachel decided to play along. Little did she know that the sexy rodeo rogue was playing for keeps!

MILLION DOLLAR SWEEPSTAKES

SWP-M96

Welcome to the

Miramar Inn

A new series
by Carol Grace

This bed and breakfast offers great views, gracious hospitality—and possibly even love!

You've already met proprietors Mandy and Adam Gray in LONELY MILLIONAIRE (Jan. '95). Now this happily married pair invite you to stay and share the romantic stories of how two other very special couples found love at the Miramar Inn:

ALMOST A HUSBAND—Carrie Stephens needed a fiancé—fast! And her partner, Matt Graham, was only too happy to accommodate, but could he let Carrie go when their charade ended?

AVAILABLE SEPTEMBER 1995

ALMOST MARRIED—Laurie Clayton was eager to baby-sit her precocious goddaughter—but she hadn't counted on Cooper Buckingham playing "daddy"!

AVAILABLE MARCH 1996

Don't miss these charming stories coming soon from

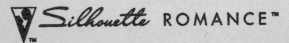

Silhouette ROMANCE™

Yo amo novelas con corazón!

Starting this March, Harlequin opens up to a whole new world of readers with two new romance lines in SPANISH!

Harlequin Deseo
* passionate, sensual and exciting stories

Harlequin Bianca
* romances that are fun, fresh and very contemporary

With four titles a month, each line will offer the same wonderfully romantic stories that you've come to love—now available in Spanish.

Look for them at selected retail outlets.

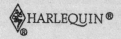 HARLEQUIN®

As seen on TV!
Free Gift Offer

With a Free Gift proof-of-purchase from any Silhouette® book,
you can receive a beautiful cubic zirconia pendant.

This gorgeous marquise-shaped stone is a genuine cubic
zirconia—accented by an 18" gold tone necklace.

(Approximate retail value $19.95)

Send for yours today...
compliments of *Silhouette*®

To receive your free gift, a cubic zirconia pendant, send us one original proof-of-purchase, photocopies not accepted, from the back of any Silhouette Romance™, Silhouette Desire®, Silhouette Special Edition®, Silhouette Intimate Moments® or Silhouette Shadows™ title available in February, March or April at your favorite retail outlet, together with the Free Gift Certificate, plus a check or money order for $1.75 U.S./$2.25 CAN. (do not send cash) to cover postage and handling, payable to Silhouette Free Gift Offer. We will send you the specified gift. Allow 6 to 8 weeks for delivery. Offer good until April 30, 1996 or while quantities last. Offer valid in the U.S. and Canada only.

Free Gift Certificate

Name: _____

Address: _____

City: _____ State/Province: _____ Zip/Postal Code: _____

Mail this certificate, one proof-of-purchase and a check or money order for postage and handling to: SILHOUETTE FREE GIFT OFFER 1996. In the U.S.: 3010 Walden Avenue, P.O. Box 9057, Buffalo NY 14269-9057. In Canada: P.O. Box 622, Fort Erie,

FREE GIFT OFFER   079-KBZ-R
ONE PROOF-OF-PURCHASE
To collect your fabulous FREE GIFT, a cubic zirconia pendant, you must include this original proof-of-purchase for each gift with the properly completed Free Gift Certificate.

079-KBZ-R

You're About to Become a

Privileged Woman

Reap the rewards of fabulous free gifts and benefits with proofs-of-purchase from Silhouette and Harlequin books

Pages & Privileges™

It's our way of thanking you for buying our books at your favorite retail stores.

PROOF OF PURCHASE

SR-PP114

Offer expires October 31, 1996

Pages & Privileges ™

**Harlequin and Silhouette—
the most privileged readers in the world!**

For more information about Harlequin and Silhouette's PAGES & PRIVILEGES program call the Pages & Privileges Benefits Desk: 1-503-794-2499

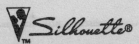

Silhouette®

SR-PP114